TWENTY-ONE KILLS

LEAP LIMIT BOOK 2

JANICE BOEKHOFF

Lost Canyon
PRESS

P.O. Box 624
Bettendorf, IA 52722

Trade Paperback ISBN: 978-1-948003-14-8
Ebook ISBN: 978-1-948003-13-1
Cover by Kim Mesman (mesmandesignco.com)

Mars Lockporte thought he'd tamed the time travel beast by leaping home in one piece after spending twenty-one hours in the Civil War and saving his best friend in the process. But even though Kiefer is now alive, Mars can't rejoice. Somehow, his actions have eliminated Liam Crosby, the third member of their trio. Before Mars can figure out why, the impossible happens—he's pulled back into the past against his will ... and comes face-to-face with a killer.

Indeed, history is nothing more than a tableau of crimes and misfortunes.
—Voltaire

If time is a wave, then it's theoretically possible to leap from one wave crest to another.
—Mars Lockporte, draft of doctoral thesis

PROLOGUE

Denver Coliseum, Denver, Colorado
February 13, 2046

Liam Crosby and I met on the night my father conned his way out of prison. The championship basketball game was my last high school basketball experience, and I didn't even play. I sat in the first row of spectators behind the bench, in awe of Liam, the sharpshooter on the Boulder Panthers team. Every time the point guard got the ball to him, he launched up a shot that almost always went in the hoop.

The crowd roared its approval, at least the Panther fans did. Somehow, the chaotic mass of yelling spectators didn't bother Liam. In fact, he catered to them, hyping up his hometown's fans with a small dance after each three-point basket and egging on the opposing team's boos with a military-style salute as he ran back down the court.

My team, the Fossil Ridge Sabercats from Fort Collins, didn't make it this far in the tournament, but the high school athletic association enjoyed my aggressive style of play enough to place me on the ceremonial All-Star Team. Thus, I had front row access to this game.

It was technically my senior year of high school, though I turned sixteen that March, because I'd completed a full year of classes during each semester. Other than my participation in sports, high school had been about as exciting as watching the Weather Channel on mute—the same people yapping away trying to show how smart they are. Most of my fellow students couldn't back up their boasting.

By the end of the game, Liam had scored thirty-six points—a personal record—and the Panthers won the championship title. His coach set up a celebration dinner at the hotel where all the players were staying, and he even invited the All-Star players.

Over mediocre pizza, Liam and I talked about anime and gaming. His parents had just bought him the first version of the holographic game Legend of Zelda: Quantum Horizon for his birthday. The game used cards, barely a quarter-inch thick, from which a quantum projector displayed six-foot-tall holographic images of the characters. They battled each other based on the players' body movements. He promised to show me the next day before we left to go back to our separate towns.

We talked late into the night, eventually moving from the lobby to dip our feet in the pool. The topics ranged from classes to pets to what college would be like. He even told me about how he was adopted, and though he loves his adoptive parents, he longed to track down his birth parents someday.

As our easy conversation wound down, Liam cleared his throat. "Hey, Mars, uh, I know this is a weird thing to ask about, but some of the guys were saying your dad is in prison."

That wasn't actually a question, but my heart pounded anyway. Every time my dad came up, I pushed down a basket-ball-sized swell of guilt. I first realized my dad was different when I was six because I asked my mom why Dad was allowed to lie, but I wasn't. She gave me a lecture on staying away from bad people. As if I could stay away from my own father. But Liam doesn't need to know all my baggage.

"Yeah, he's been there for about eight years." I swallowed hard before admitting, "I turned him in."

"You what?"

Was he surprised that I volunteered the information or that I sent my own father to prison? I pushed down another ball of shame before I spoke. "My father wrote a book claiming I was the youngest person to battle early onset dementia at the age of eight. He said he discovered the cure—a blend of herbs only he knew. Then he asked people to send money for my medical care and to purchase the herbs to help their loved ones. It was a double dip of fraud. Help my kid by donating and buying worthless herbs you could grow in your own backyard. I knew it was wrong, so I talked to my cousin about it." At fourteen years old, Rochelle was the oldest nonparental figure I had. "She told me to tell the school counselor, who then got the police involved." I kicked my feet, sending a spray of water arcing through the air. "It was my fault they sent him away."

"Yep."

Liam's flat statement caused my stomach to drop and my shoulders to hunch. He must think I'm an awful person. How could I have done that to my own father? "At least I didn't have to face him at trial. I testified via recorded hologram. His lawyer questioned me without him there."

Liam kicked water in my direction. "You did what you had to."

I took a deep breath, but my shoulders wouldn't relax. "I didn't want to."

"Of course not."

His simple acceptance diffused my guilt like dandelion seeds blown in the wind. My mother had told me the same thing, but I couldn't believe her. If she truly thought it was the right thing to do, she would have turned him in herself.

Half an hour later, we took the stairs up to our rooms. Liam left me at the fifth floor to go to the room he was sharing with his dad. As I headed up the next flight of stairs to my empty room, my shoulders finally released their tension.

I had done what I had to do. The *right* thing. I wasn't at all like my father.

At my room, I swiped the key on my phone, and the lock turned green to allow me inside. I was still too young to get an implanted CRASH—Currency, Risk Assessment, and Honesty—device on the inside of my elbow, which would act as a key. At eighteen, most people got one to help with paying for goods and services, though the device was optional.

I pushed hard against the door since this one was difficult to open. But then I hesitated. The interior was dark. I remembered leaving the light on. Had the housekeeper been in here?

Strong hands grabbed my sweatshirt and dragged me inside a few feet before slamming me against the wall. The door to my room banged shut.

A small amount of light filtered in from an open door connecting my room to the room next door. An assistant coach from my school, who was acting as my chaperone, was staying in that connected room. I was supposed to let him know when I got back.

But it wasn't the assistant coach in front of me.

Dark hair. Dark eyes that could be deep green, though it was too dark to be sure. Two inches taller than my six foot, three inches. *My father.*

One glance through the open door from this angle told me what happened to the coach. He was lying motionless between the two Queen beds.

Why was my father here? The superficial characteristics of dark hair and green eyes were where our resemblance ended. I have my mom's high brows and cheekbones. Plus, a thicker jaw and wider shoulders. If I could bring myself to fight against him, it would have been anyone's guess who'd win.

My father pressed his forearm into my chest, driving the breath from my lungs.

"Didn't expect to see me, *son*?"

"How ...?"

He leaned close, within inches of my face. I turned my head away. His hot breath warmed my cheek as he laughed. "Why would you ask 'how'? I can convince anyone to do anything."

True, his powers of persuasion were almost supernatural. Adrenaline flooded my system, a welcome sensation, but then, the truth squelched the energetic effects of the chemical cocktail. My father was here. Prison couldn't hold him.

But I wasn't eight years old anymore.

I shoved him off me. "Why are you here?"

"Now that's a better question." He held up my driver's license. "I came for this. And you."

His plan came to me quickly as if we shared a devious mind. We might look similar, but he couldn't pass for a sixteen-year-old. Instead, he would use me to make whatever scheme he came up with sound more legitimate. Same as before.

He moved closer to the bed and softened his voice. "When I saw you on the witness stand, it gutted me."

A small spark of hope flared in my heart. Did that mean he realized what he'd done was wrong? No. I stomped out the ember. If he was a changed man, he'd be faithfully serving his time, not skulking around my hotel room and knocking out my coach. Hopefully, my coach was only unconscious.

"You owe me," he said while flipping the license through his fingers. "How could you testify against your own father?"

There it was. The true Sean Lockporte. Everyone existed to either further his goals or make his life easier.

I tried to grab my license, but he whipped it behind his back.

Anger replaced my hope, condensing into a tight ball in my chest. "I guess I testified because my father is a snotpocket who preys on other people."

I leaned around him, still reaching for my ID. If I had the CRASH implant, I wouldn't even need it, though most people still took them on long trips. Technology wasn't infallible.

Speaking of elbows, my father had a strange black band encircling his. Probably a signal blocker. The government claimed they couldn't track a particular person with the CRASH devices, but of course they could.

Just as my fingers grazed my license, he rammed a fist into my sternum, catching me completely off guard and throwing me back into the wall. I stared at him open-mouthed. Despite his failings, he'd never hit me before.

A knock on the door jolted me from my shock.

My father and I turned as one. Who would be knocking at midnight?

"Mars, I need to talk to you. Something has happened."

Liam.

"You're sure this is his room?" another voice rasped.

Liam's dad? They were obviously trying to get my attention without waking the occupants of the rooms around me.

"It's the room number he gave me." A second knock, this one harder. "Mars, it's important."

This was my chance. I called out, "I'm here. Just give me a minute." Then, I planted my feet and glared at my father. "I'm not going anywhere with you. You'd better get out of here before they suspect something."

He gave a low frustrated growl as he backed toward the connecting door. His gaze darted back and forth between me and his escape. He still clutched my driver's license in his fist, but so what? Let him have it.

As I opened the door for Liam and his dad, I heard a click from the outside door of the room next to mine. My father was getting away. But he was too dangerous to send Liam's dad after him. I wouldn't put them in danger. Besides, we had to get help for my coach.

Liam began rambling about how he hated to tell me this, but he had news about my father.

I put up a hand to stop him. "I know. We need to call the police. My father just left."

CHAPTER 1

University of Colorado Boulder
September 20, 2051
10:17 a.m.
21 hours after Mars returned from the Civil War

Torri Clavinger swipes a hand through the empty space where a person should be. The bare walls of the office surround her like gray sentinels, bearing witness to an event they couldn't voice. Neither could she.

Two minutes ago, Mars Lockporte stood just in front of the trellis scaffolding on the side wall. His wavy dark hair had been a little askew from running his hand through it. His eyes had lit up like sea-green emeralds while he talked about his work. Until Akane Souza came in. Then, those enchanting eyes narrowed and darkened.

But before he could find out what Akane wanted, he'd gone. He just disappeared. The seemingly solid cells of his body flickered like a dying light bulb, then finally blinked out of existence. Impossible, and yet she saw it happen.

Before leaving the office, Akane said if Torri told anyone, no one would believe it. Which is probably true. Even in her own head, it sounds ridiculous.

But the words scrolling over his screensaver seem to confirm it: *A leap in time requires a leap in logic.* She glances at the sticky note stuck to the bottom corner of the monitor where she'd rewritten the sentiment. *A leap in time requires a leap in faith.*

Where did he leap to? The law of conservation of mass comes to mind from her physics classes in high school. Matter can change forms, but it can't be created or destroyed. So, Mars has changed forms? Or maybe just changed location?

A sigh leaks from her lips. Standing here will not spontaneously cause her to figure this out. And it's clear that chasing after Akane won't be any help. But Torri has one more way to gain information—the guy who'd come in just afterward, looking for Mars.

Two steps out the door, she nearly runs into a handsome older man who is focused on a paper in his hand. He mutters an apology before recognizing that she doesn't belong here.

"I'm Dr. Pearce. You're not one of my grad students."

"No. I'm Torri." She stops herself before her official title rolls off her tongue. Best not to tell him she's a police officer. Even a mere animal control officer tends to make people nervous, like her very presence means they are doing something wrong. "I was visiting someone."

"Can I help you find them?"

"Well, I came to see Mars, but he isn't here."

Dr. Pearce frowns, and his thick brows hide his eyes, but not before she sees a flicker of understanding in them.

A shiver courses through her. He knows something about what's going on. She rushes to ask, "Do you have any idea when he'll be back?"

He answers slowly, deliberately. "No. I need to see him myself when he returns. I'd try later in the day if I were you."

Later in the day. Similar to the last time she'd been looking for Mars when he was MIA. Interesting.

"Okay. In that case, I'll pop in to see Ellis. Where does he sit?"

Dr. Pearce gestures to a hallway on the right.

"Thanks."

When he came looking for Mars, Ellis seemed to be a friend and colleague. Maybe he knows something.

As she approaches an open office door, she sees legs sticking out from under the desk. She gives a soft knock on the doorframe.

With a thump against the desk, Ellis rises, rubbing the back of his blond head.

"Sorry. Didn't mean to surprise you."

His eyes widen with interest. Good. Maybe he'll be willing to give her some answers. But first, she needs to get him talking. Fortunately, that's one of her specialties. "What are you working on?"

"Temporal phenomena."

She crosses her arms over her chest and leans sideways against the door jamb. "Same nonanswer that Mars gave me. Care to elaborate?"

He bites his lip as if he's not supposed to elaborate. Then, he gestures for her to come farther into the room. Why not? He's a scrawny five-seven. Several inches shorter than her and no match for her police training. She moves inside and closes the door behind her.

"Mine's a little different from Mars's, and yet similar."

She smiles. "Spoken like a nuanced nerd."

This gets a laugh. "Mine is more, uh, I guess you could say paranormal. I'm trying to determine if dreams are temporally predictive."

"What?"

"Basically, I want to find out if people leap ahead in time when they are in an unconscious state. It would explain so many instances of déjà vu."

"I have always wondered why people experience déjà vu."

He gives her a toothy grin. "You can volunteer for my study.

It involves being hooked up to Dreamcatcher, a device that reads brainwaves and renders them in 3D on a monitor to display the dreams." He dips his head slightly. "Actually, it's Mars's device —one he's currently having patent issues with—but I'm doing the real work, running the statistics to determine the predictive accuracy of dreams. You'd just have to come sleep for me."

She twists her lips to the side. "Really? I don't think we know each other that well."

His pale skin flames red. "That sounded more suggestive than I intended."

Or perhaps that's exactly what he intended. "I'll consider it. Hey, what do you know about Mars's current project?"

"He's also working on—"

"Temporal phenomena. Yeah, I got that. Do you know what that means?"

The most basic interview procedure taught to her by the police academy: don't ask for information directly. Merely ask if they know. Everyone wants to be in the know. Once they admit they know something, it becomes much harder to hold information back.

Ellis sinks into a rolling chair with a sigh. Unlike Mars, he has another chair for visitors, which he gestures at. Torri sits, keeping a relaxed posture so as not to seem like she's interrogating him.

"I don't know exactly what his method is because he keeps things close, but he's working on entangling himself with quantum wave packets."

"For what reason?"

He bites his lip. It's all the answer she needs.

"To travel in time." The awe in her voice surprises her. It's what she suspected. And yet it's still too unbelievable.

Ellis leans forward to put his elbows on his knees. "Your turn. Did he do it? Is that where he's gone?"

Despite the utter shock crowding her mind, Torri manages to

adopt a practiced detachment in her voice. "All evidence points to that."

Bitterroot Mountains, Montana
August 30, 1972

I LAND on my hands and knees in the heart of a thick bush with branches scratching at my exposed arms and poking through my T-shirt. Thankfully, there are no thorns.

Breathe in through the nose. Out through the mouth. I need to refill my lungs from the shock of the journey. Or maybe my lung tissue is angry from being reconstituted bit by quantum bit. Why did I leap in time again?

One minute, I'm in my office in 2051 with a gorgeous animal control officer and a devious grad student, and the next minute, I'm out here in the middle of nowhere. No quasicrystal to guide me—the only thing gripped in my fist is my cell phone. Who knows if it works after the trip.

I wasn't even under the trellis, which serves to vibrate my quantum signature to the Fibonacci pulse. I suppose I was somewhat close to the trellis. But how would it know where and when to send me?

To leave like that ... ugh, what must Torri have thought when I faded from view? I shake my head to focus on the here and now. I need to know what I'm dealing with.

It's pitch black. When I turn my head, I see a swath of stars blanketing the sky above. I must be out in nature, away from city lights. But where am I? Better question, *when* am I?

Rustling sounds come from behind me. Please, no bobcats or Confederate cannons this time.

I crawl forward out of the bush, making noise even while trying not to. The rustling could also be a bear or a mountain lion. I have no way to know what part of the US I'm in or if I'm even in the country at all.

The dark shapes of spruce trees loom in front of me, reminding me a little of Boulder. What I wouldn't give to go back to my home right now. *Now.* Such an easy concept for everyone but me. In trying to "fix" my now by leaping back in time to save one friend—Kiefer—I eliminated another friend's life—Liam. I'm supposed to be in my office entertaining Torri while figuring out how to get Liam back.

My mind puts its primary protest in the background, on repeat—this shouldn't be possible. And yet, here I am.

I peek around the rear of the bush into what appears to be a clearing. Someone sweeps a flashlight in my direction, illuminating multiple thickets of trees and brush around me. I squint until the beam angles downward. It reflects off something lying on the ground that barely registers in my consciousness. An ice-cold shiver races down my spine.

Is that a body? Maybe the low light is playing tricks on me.

Beyond the cone of light, this person's movements would be visible without the help of the flashlight. A gauzy white halo surrounds the figure, including the overcoat and hat he is wearing. At least, I think it's a man.

I let out a deep sigh. *Not again.*

On my first leap in time, I encountered a man with the same innocent-looking halo in the middle of a deadly Civil War battle. Now, I'm once again confronted by a halo-encased man, except there's no battle going on here and he seems to have a body at his feet. This could be something far more sinister.

A muted notification pings from my phone. Thankfully, the sound comes at the same time that this person steps on a stick. He must not have heard it. I quickly put the phone on silent. The notification is from the quantum wave detector app I created to notify me of fluctuations in quantum phenomena. It measures the percentage of superimposed waves in the surrounding area, using fifty percent as the average relative background for wave activity. Notifications come only when the percentage rises above seventy-five. The screen shows eighty-five percent of the localized quantum waves are superimposed upon each other. Could that have something to do with why I traveled?

The person's light beam swings in the opposite direction, toward the ground behind him. Thank goodness my phone automatically went to its dimmest setting. I must be in a time period more recent than the Civil War, since they didn't have flashlights then.

For the first time, the air temperature registers. It's cold, maybe around forty-five degrees Fahrenheit. My bare arms are peppered with goosebumps.

A strange smell permeates the air. Something between rotting garbage and raw sewage with oddly fruity undertones. I put my hand over my nose to block the stench.

The beam continues moving, not landing on anything in particular. Perhaps I was mistaken. Did I really see someone lying on the ground? It could be a trick of the light. But the smell …

I fixate on the beam until it revisits that particular area.

The light sweeps over a shoulder clad in a cotton shirt. And then a neck with what looks like hair splayed out near it. No mistaking it—a human form lies sprawled in a pile of fallen leaves, unmoving. A woman, judging by the size. Unlike the man, she's not wearing a coat. Dark patches are splattered across her light-colored shirt. Is that blood?

I choke on my own spit.

The flashlight sweeps to my bush, blinding me. Can he see me through the branches? I hold my breath, not daring to move. Thankfully, my phone is clutched to my chest and my elbow is tight against my side, hiding my CRASH device. It should have automatically dimmed as well, but after my previous leap, it flipped out on me by displaying a strange polka-dot pattern, not something I want this guy to see.

He takes several steps in my direction, then a sharp, angry

howl comes from my left. He shifts to the side, distracted by the sound. A coyote maybe? Or a wolf? But it doesn't sound like any coyotes or wolves we have in Colorado. This howl is higher pitched.

With him distracted, I draw back to hide behind the thicker part of the bush. A haze from the flashlight filters through the branches for a few more seconds, then completely disappears. Everything goes silent. Not that the man was making much noise before.

Eventually, I peer around the bush again. The area is dark and deserted. He's gone.

I creep out and approach the body in a crouch. There isn't much moonlight, but my eyes are adjusting to the dimness. I still have my phone, except using the flashlight would attract the man's attention if he's still nearby, so I shove it in my back pocket.

Up close, the blood on her shirt coats the fabric in a dendrite design, like abstract art. But I tear my gaze away from her clothing to focus on her face. Slack and expressionless. She's clearly dead. Probably has been for hours.

She's about my age, around twenty, maybe even a little younger, with a petite frame and long auburn hair. The side of her face has deep bruising along her left cheek. But the massive amount of blood came from a slash in her throat.

No blood is flowing now. It has congealed along the sides of her neck like tiny rivers streaming into her hair.

My stomach roils at the sight. Even as horrible as this is, she is not the source of the smell. I raise my gaze, and it lands on another body a few feet away, farther out into the clearing. I sit back on my heels and identify another suspiciously human-sized lump a few feet past that one.

This clearing is used as a graveyard. How many victims are in this area?

Every muscle in my body tenses, and I push back into my crouch as if I can spring to my feet and run from this. I've leaped into an unknown time in the middle of a killing ground.

The man with the halo is probably a serial killer. Why else would he be out here? I'll have to rethink my theory on the halos. Originally, on my one and only leap, the halo was attached to the best man I've ever met. But this situation seems to be in the reverse, where the halo surrounds a despicable man. If my original leap limit holds true, I'll have twenty-one hours to try to figure this out—and survive—in this time period before I leap back.

My heart races into overdrive as I process the details of this scene. I'm an adrenaline junkie, so these chemical surges aren't new to me, but the fear of my own death is what normally drives it. Not being confronted with the deaths of innocent women.

Mars, get it together. Falling apart here is too risky.

"Hey," a deep voice says behind me, followed by the telltale click of a gun.

I turn in my crouch to find someone shining a flashlight in my eyes. It must be Halo Man.

"Stand."

My legs were starting to burn anyway. As I rise, my phone falls to the ground, face up. I must not have shoved it far enough into my pocket.

I reach for it, but he yells, "Hands up!"

I comply, leaving the phone on the ground.

He ignores it for the moment, instead asking, "How did you get here?"

The short answer would be *I have no idea*, because I'm not supposed to be here. The long answer would involve quantum signatures plus the wave-particle duality of time and would likely get me shot. He's probably just asking how I got to this remote area. "Um, I walked."

"You walked into the mountains wearing a T-shirt?" He sounds raspy. Is he trying to disguise his voice?

I look down at my chest. My Ms. Pac-Man T-shirt with two

cartoon ghosts on it—Inky and Blinky—somehow fits with the way an invisible ghost seems to have been directing my leaps. Why the Civil War? And why here? And while we're at it, why am I always confronted by men with guns?

"What is that?" He directs the beam toward my phone.

"Uh, a powerful flashlight."

Now that he's turned the beam downward, I catch a shadow of his face. Only enough to register a strong nose and chin framed by shaggy brown hair. He has taken off his hat. He pushes the hair off his forehead and holds it, like he's thinking. There's something strange about his right ear. It's thick and deformed. Maybe he's a wrestler?

His coat sleeve pulls up a little, exposing a glinting gold watch. The flashlight swings back to me, and I'm blinded again.

"Pick it up."

I go down on one knee and grab my phone. The screen lights up, displaying my screensaver—a picture of my wolf hybrid curled up on her doggy bed.

"What is—"

His question breaks off as I flip the flashlight on full power and direct it at his face. Thank God it works after the leap. The beam is twice as bright as his flashlight.

I did warn him.

Before he can recover, I arc my body to the side, keeping the flashlight in his eyes. He fires at where the light is, but the bullet buzzes past my rib cage.

Since he won't be able to tell depth perception with the light coming at him head on, my safest course of action is to go right at him. I advance to within a few feet from him.

Rather than trying to get the gun away and having it go off, I take my chance to escape. I shove his shoulder from the side, knocking him to the ground, then I flick my flashlight off and run at an angle toward the trees.

He fires wildly in the direction he thinks I went, but his eyes haven't adjusted yet.

I slip into the tree line and take long quiet steps for about ten feet. Then I crouch down to hide behind a grouping of gnarled trees with several vines forming a curtain around them. I shove my phone between my knees and again keep my left elbow tight to my body to ensure that my implanted CRASH device doesn't emit enough light to give me away. Even though it has automatically dimmed due to the low light, it's still glowing a deep mulberry color to signify high risk and low reward.

This forest is dense. He won't find me in the dark with his dinky flashlight. Besides, if he gets too close, I can see his body halo.

From the thrashing noises to my left, he doesn't know how to hunt effectively in the forest. But he's closer than I'd like. I keep my breathing shallow and quiet.

Several minutes later, a frustrated yell comes from farther away.

Then, that blasted coyote howls again. The animal could track me much more easily than Halo Man, but that seems unlikely.

I stay put, controlling my breathing and silently listening. At least twenty more minutes go by with no sounds.

He's given up. And the cold is creeping into my limbs. Time for me to move.

If there is one thing I learned in my first and only time leap, it's how to navigate in the forest quietly. As long as I keep checking for sounds around me and for the body halo in the distance, I'll be able to avoid him.

Unless he also sees a body halo on me. It's a possibility I haven't considered before. But no matter what, I can't stay here. The sky is already lightening with the first hint of dawn. I won't be able to hide forever. And no doubt, he'll be coming back.

CHAPTER 2

THE COLD HOLDS me hostage as I trudge through the woods for at least an hour. If I stop, I'll just get colder. I rub my arms again to warm my bare skin. The sun emits a pinkish glow to the east, but not enough to light my way yet.

Besides, the dark has been my refuge. If it's hard for me to see, it's hard for Halo Man to see too. A fair fight with him, minus the gun, could go either way. I've been in plenty of fist fights. This guy is shorter, but he's also stockier. And possibly a wrestler. Whenever I get home, I need to brush up on my defensive skills. I barely remember how to perform a roundhouse kick from my Tae Kwon Do classes in first grade. Oddly enough, I quit the sport because the main focus of our dojo was to learn the proper form, meaning I didn't get to hit or kick kids very often. The adrenaline seeking part of me moved on to flag football. As long as I was making a play for the flag, everyone overlooked a clean tackle.

Except tackling a guy with a gun probably wouldn't have ended well. I need someone to train me in disarming an assailant. Maybe someone like a police officer. Even if she's in the animal control division, Torri must have had some self-defense training. An image of her dark hair, bronze-colored skin, and light brown cashmere eyes floods me with another kind of chemical cocktail. But then, I picture her face as I last saw it— eyes wide with shock, brows high and pinched together. She saw me leap. She would suspect this is why I was gone before. What does she think happened to me?

Oh crap. Akane Souza was there too. She'll probably tell Torri everything. Who knows what Torri will think about me screwing around with history.

At least this time, it wasn't my choice. Somehow, that doesn't make it better. I must have done something to set this whole leap-limit cycle in motion. Something that I don't know how to undo.

I grope for my phone in my back pocket as if it has the answers to why this is happening, but I brush my fingers against the plastic case without bringing it out. Although Halo Man doesn't seem to be anywhere around, it's best not to take the chance of being seen by the light of my phone. And it will be no help at all. After my last leap, I could have downloaded some historical information into a quarto—an efficient data storage system—but I didn't plan to travel again until I was ready. If I make it home, that's the first thing I'll do.

The thought of my home time brings another sinking realization. My father's parole hearing is set to happen later today. Sometime in the afternoon. I can't remember the exact time, but I'm sure to miss it during this leap. Despite the guilt still plaguing me due to testifying against him, I believe prison is the best place for him so he can't ruin more lives. Without my presence to protest his release, he's sure to con the parole board. I have no choice but to file that under Hidden Casualties of Time Travel.

How far have I walked? Probably over a mile, at least. Two, maybe? It's hard to tell in the rough up and down terrain.

A pinpoint of something in the distance makes me squint. It's a light source. Not that far away, barely visible through the multitude of branches. Could be a house or cabin of some sort.

I head in that direction, staying as quiet as possible. This leap is so different from my time in the Civil War, yet I'm still slinking through a dark forest trying not to run into an enemy. The chill causes me to fantasize about the seventy-degree days in 1862 West Virginia. With a little luck, things should warm up once the sun rises.

When I'm halfway to whatever the light source is, I catch a glimpse of a shadow moving to my right. My pulse picks up as the shadow slides along with my movements, except it's not my shadow. I'm being stalked. Too big to be a big cat.

Someone besides Halo Man is out here.

At the next wide tree that I pass, I step behind the trunk and wait for two seconds before I move again.

A figure cautiously peeks around, but I've circled behind them.

"Who are you?" I demand.

The person jumps and lands facing me. A grizzled man with a bald head and a five o'clock shadow on his cheeks and chin. He has on a leather coat, and a backpack is slung over one shoulder. He holds a fedora-style hat in one hand, but no weapons. This guy looks like some kind of Indiana Jones wannabe.

He grunts and darts away, heading deeper into the woods in a direction perpendicular to the line I've been walking. I almost call out to him but think better of it. He was following me without a word, which means he might be out here for nefarious reasons. Of course, he could have followed me because he wondered what I'm doing out here in the middle of the night, rightfully so.

I continue on toward the light until I reach the edge of a small clearing. A rustic log cabin sits in the middle of it with one light shining from inside. It's a surprisingly big structure for as remote as this area seems. The clearing doesn't appear to be natural. More like a giant swung a club around in a perfect ten-foot circle to clear the trees on every degree of the arc. Several stumps stick up in random places, but mostly the terrain is lumpy ground. A seven-foot-high wood pile answers the question regarding the ultimate fate of those trees.

Near the corner of the cabin, a roughly square object is covered with a tarp. Some sort of utility vehicle? The vehicle sits on gravel, as if there's a driveway around front.

A loud howl from my right startles me. It's resonating and mournful, not sharp like the one I heard earlier. A beagle mix crouches with its paws down in front and its rear end sticking up in the air. Perhaps a playful stance or perhaps a warning. The dog's coloring resembles a beagle but with the added mottling of a blue heeler. Plus, the animal is obviously a mix due to its unusual height. It stands three feet tall and looks like it weighs over fifty pounds. The dog rises to its full height, then crouches into the same position again.

"Don't move," a deep voice from my left commands.

The dog starts to growl. At me? Or at the person over my shoulder?

I glance behind to find a man with a weapon and a flashlight, both pointed at my chest. Not the same man, at least, since he doesn't have a body halo.

"Hands in the air," he says.

The flashlight beam rises to my face. He's trying to blind me to get me to comply.

"Okay." I raise my arms with my palms out.

He takes a step closer. "What is that?"

I scan my body before realizing he's talking about the low-level glow from my implant. The CRASH device allows me to pay for things in my time period, assess activities by risk, and prove my honesty. It flashes different colors in different modes, none of which this guy is likely to understand. From the corner of my eye, I see the Risk Assessment mode is flashing a bright shade of grape, which is a mixture of high risk—deep red—and unknown reward—medium blue.

"Uh, it's a tattoo." Good thing it's not on the Honesty setting, otherwise it would change colors and give away its true function.

"It seems to glow."

"Probably a trick of the light." I point at his flashlight, and he lowers it a bit.

The man is in his mid to upper thirties and is dressed in a park ranger's uniform. Slacks, button-down shirt under an open suit coat, all in dark green with a black, tucked-in tie. Not a great color if anyone hunts in this area. They should have made their uniforms bright orange.

His physique is intimidating. He's a few inches shorter than my height of six-three, but where I'm naturally muscular, he's lumberjack strong. What's even more intimidating is his long-barreled shotgun. "Name?"

"Mars Lockporte."

The man gives me a double take, like most do upon hearing my odd moniker. "What are you doing out here?"

The dog has come to sit by my right leg. He or she nudges my fingers with a wet nose, so I scratch the soft fur on top of its head with one hand. The other I keep at half mast so he doesn't consider shooting me. "Out for a nature walk with my dog."

"That's not your dog." He sounds suspicious but with a hint of amusement. "She's been hanging around here for the last several days. Won't seem to move on. I call her Daisy because she rolls in the daisy blooms right before she eats them."

I give her head a pat. "Well, maybe if you would give her some food, she wouldn't have to eat flowers."

"No can do. Against policy to feed the wildlife."

"Does she look like wildlife?"

"Not as much as you do. So, what are you doing here?"

I let out a long sigh, buying time to make something up. "My girlfriend and I drove up here to have some quiet time. We got into a fight, and she kicked me out of the car."

"Then, why aren't you near the road?"

This guy, and his twenty questions. "I went into the woods

thinking it was a shortcut back to town." There has to be a town around here somewhere, right? Time to turn the tables on him. "Are you a park ranger? Where are we exactly?"

The man lowered his shotgun, resting the stock in the dirt. "You're in the Sula Ranger District of the Bitterroot National Forest, outside Meadowlark. This isn't the main ranger station that you can see from the road. And if you're trying to get back to Meadowlark, you're going in the wrong direction. Did you come from Salmon or Missoula?"

Not sure what Salmon is, but Missoula sounds familiar. It might be near Idaho or Montana. I'm vaguely familiar with the area from my genealogy research. My father has some family originating in Idaho, near the border of Montana.

I'm spared from answering by the sound of an approaching vehicle. Daisy hides behind my leg at the noise.

The growling crunch of tires comes from the tree line to my right. In the rise of dawn over the last few minutes, a gravel trail is now visible, about half the width of a road.

An all-terrain vehicle breaks from the trees and skids to a stop in front of the tarp-covered mound. The woman on the vehicle wears a similar uniform but with a cravat-type neck piece instead of a tie.

"Rasher, you haven't been answering your radio," she says.

"Nice of you to notice, but you didn't need to come all the way out here. I can handle whatever comes up." His tone says he wants or needs the chance to prove himself. Maybe he hasn't been on the job long.

I peer at him again. About thirty-five, but with no middle-aged paunch. His light brown hair is neatly trimmed above his ears. His name tag labels him as Marvin Rasher.

The woman plants her hands on her hips. Her strawberry-blond hair is pulled back in tight braids that hint at darker, perhaps more coppery roots. "Then why haven't you radioed for backup since you obviously have an intruder?"

Rasher rolls his eyes. "This isn't an intruder. This is Mars."

"And my name's Venus." She bats her eyes in a sarcastic way. When I don't respond, she follows up with, "Did your parents really name you after a rocky clump of nothing?"

I bristle at her condescending tone. She doesn't look much older than me, yet her superior air makes her seem world-wise. The kind of woman who takes control in every situation. There aren't too many time periods in the past when a strong woman would be accepted as an equal. She must face a lot of opposition, especially if she's the boss.

"Um, Miss …" She doesn't have a name tag. There's only a gray-green rectangle where it should be located.

With a scowl, she says, "Not Miss anything. Park Ranger Brenda Morrow."

Morrow. That name sounds vaguely familiar.

Yep, definitely has a chip on her shoulder. "Okay then." I clear my throat. "Rangers Morrow and Rasher, I found something that I need to show you."

"You sure we should be going northwest?" Ranger Morrow asks with an edge to her voice. "And what are we looking for? It's too early in the morning for a wild goose chase."

Though I've given her only vague directions, she plows ahead of the two of us. If the dark bags under her eyes are any indication, she didn't sleep well last night either. Could explain her irritation. Or perhaps that's due to my fuzzy recollection of where we're going.

I'm wide awake, though. My biological clock thinks it's early afternoon, probably. I don't have my grandfather's watch, having lost it on my last leap. I could check my phone, which would still be set on my home time, except then I'd have no way to explain its existence to these two park rangers in whatever time period we are in. I'm guessing it's the last half of the twentieth century, but I can't narrow it down yet.

Ranger Morrow wanted to use an ATV to find the site, but I told her I needed to walk to be sure I could find my way back to it. The exertion could also account for her grumpy attitude.

"How do we know this isn't some sort of trap?"

Her question is directed at Rasher. He, too, seems unsure about following a stranger who will only say this site is important to law enforcement. Even so, he stays silent.

"I think it's just to the south a bit." I pull the blanket they gave me for warmth tighter around myself.

The day is starting to warm up, but it's still in the fifties. Not to mention the cold emanating from the glances Morrow is still throwing at me. I don't even have Daisy to act as a buffer. She ran off in a different direction as soon as we entered the woods.

Things look much different in the daylight. Less threatening, but the forest feels more imposing, maybe because of all the trees towering over us that I navigated through but couldn't see last night. If I don't find the site soon, these two will think I was hallucinating.

Once we find the scene, they should initiate some kind of crime scene investigation. Though it might be limited, depending on the technology of this time. Of course, they won't have instantaneous DNA analysis like we have in 2051. They might not have any DNA analysis.

I'm not an expert in ranger uniforms, so there's no way for me to tell the decade from their clothing. Maybe if they could give me some current events?

"Can you believe what the president said yesterday?" I ask.

"What's that?" Rasher's flat tone indicates he couldn't care less. "I don't have a TV in that shack."

"You know, the thing about the economy."

"Don't listen to anything a politician says." Morrow leads us through a group of thick trees. "Especially Tricky Dick."

Ah, Richard Nixon. That means I'm probably in the early 1970s. Has Watergate happened yet? He'd gotten the nickname before the scandal, so that doesn't help narrow things down.

Morrow stops and bends over. When she stands, she's holding a man's hat, a fedora like Indiana Jones would wear. "What is this doing out here?"

"I think it belongs to the man I saw."

Morrow swivels her head around to stare at me wide-eyed. "You saw a man out here?"

I merely nod, not ready to bring up Halo Man yet. "This way." I take the lead because this area is looking familiar. With heavy steps, I navigate to my left, around the gnarled trees that hid me with their clandestine vines.

Briefly, I look back to see that Ranger Morrow has put the man's hat on her head. It's almost comical, but I'm not going to be in a laughing mood in just a few minutes.

After tracking backward using the broken branches and bent foliage from my escape, we come through a patch of trees into the clearing of death. The smell hits me first. This is much worse than the sour, sulfur-and-iron tang of blood in the Civil War battle. This is more than the smell of recent death. This is decay.

My stomach turns again at the sight in front of me, fully illuminated in—and completely contrary to—the cheery sunlight. If I'd had anything to eat in the last few hours, it would have all come up.

Female bodies are lined up in two precise, parallel rows. One row—the last victim of which I crept up to last night—consists of women about my age or a little older, spaced out roughly three feet from each other. The other row consists of neatly laid-out bodies of younger girls about half the age of the women, spaced closer to each other, only about a foot apart. All of them are redheads.

We aren't the only ones interested in them either. A half dozen vultures are feeding on the line of corpses.

Part of me wants to hightail it back to the ranger's shack and let these two stay to handle the carnage. But I was literally dropped right into the middle of this. There might be a reason for my presence.

I steel my stomach and walk down the row of women—I can't handle looking at the girls more than to just count their number. Ten little girls. The line of women is stretched out longer than the girls, but there's only nine. The last woman and girl lie at the edge of the clearing, close to where the forest takes over.

Morrow had traveled along the other side with the girls, but she's only made it halfway down. One of the deceased girls near me has a light blue scrunchie sticking out from under her neck. Hopefully, they will preserve it in case it has trace evidence. I glance back up the row at the girls and see several more scrunchies on their bodies.

Rasher still stands at the head of both lines, talking on his radio. Probably calling in the police.

A raspy hissing sound comes from inside the tree line. What could that be? Then, the same sound comes from one of the bodies a few feet away from me. I spin around to identify the source. A vulture yanks and pulls flesh from the side of one woman's face. It's the noise the vulture makes when it eats. Does that mean there are more vultures in the tree line?

My stomach does a shaky flip at that possibility. Nope, I will not get sick. I swallow down bile and step into the dark wall of trees.

As soon as the cocoon of foliage surrounds me, my phone vibrates in my pocket. Thankfully, the park rangers don't hear it. I tug it out, but it's not the notification I'd expected. This isn't reminding me to get to my father's parole hearing; it's for a meeting with a patent lawyer. *Ugh.* I'd forgotten all about that.

The government has been trying to block the patent for my new Dreamcatcher program. It closely models the human brain through the use of wave functions. My fellow graduate student, Ellis, is using the program to determine if predictive dreams are the reason for déjà vu. Apparently, the government wants it for military use, but if Dr. Pearce gets a patent on behalf of the university, they would have to pay the university for it. Instead, the government would rather claim it's too similar to another program they have developed to deserve a patent so they can work a deal with me on the side.

A week ago, this seemed like a grave miscarriage of justice aimed at the university that supports my creative PhD endeavors, but after leaping in time unintentionally with no guarantee of ever getting home, the pending legal battle doesn't register much with me.

Morrow breaks through a vine curtain a few feet away. "What's that sound?"

I shrug. "Must be the vultures."

We push farther into the trees. There's actually only one bird back here, hissing and groaning over protecting its food source.

"This is number twenty," Morrow says in a flat tone. She's probably trained to handle crises with efficiency.

This adult victim was probably the first one. Her skin is mostly gone with the exception of the thigh on one leg, which the vulture continues to pick at as though it can grab the last bits before we shoo it off. The scavenger underestimates Ranger Morrow, who rears back and kicks it away with a solid thump.

A few fragments of clothes are scattered nearby, none on the body. Several clumps of reddish-brown tufts surround her skull. Must be the remnants of her hair. Her vacant eye sockets are wide and seem to be pleading for help that will never come.

More bile rises in my throat. I take five steps to the side and throw up in the bushes. This is too much. Why did I end up here?

As I'm bent over, the blanket shifts off my shoulders and my elbow catches my eye. My CRASH device is flashing a mauve color: deep red—high risk—combined with light blue—high reward. Not a color I see often in my adrenaline junkie activities; I'm usually buried on eggplant: high risk with low reward.

Subconsciously, I must think there is value in being here. Finding the killer would get justice for these girls, but is that really what I should spend my time doing? My from-the-future goals would be better served by finding out why I leaped here in the first place. Could one of these victims be related to Seth Millstone, the man who originally killed Kiefer and whose DNA I originally entered into my time travel program?

My mind stretches that possibility out until it gets distracted by a phenomenon stemming from my last leap—a number pattern. Twenty-one hours in the past. Twenty-one hours in the present. Twenty-one stones at the Civil War hanging tree.

There are twenty victims here. This could all be a coincidence. But what if it's not? What if my leaps continue to reflect the number I chose from the Fibonacci sequence? The idea causes me to shiver with dread. If that's the case now, then we're missing a victim.

CHAPTER 3

I BACK OUT of the forest and leave Ranger Morrow in the shadows with the mostly skeletal woman. This whole scene is senseless. Not at all like the bodies of the deceased young men I saw at the Battle of Antietam. At least they died fighting for something they believed in, even if some of them were misguided. What did these women and girls die for? Just someone's sick fantasy?

There's not enough room to walk down the middle of the two rows. I circle around to the girls' side. As much as I don't want to look at what happened to them, these victims deserve my acknowledgment. They had their young lives stolen. No one has been able to recognize that before because no one had found them.

The girls are laid out very much the same as their older counterparts, but my scientific eye begins to pick out the differences. Most of the women have blood around their neck area, suggesting all their throats were cut. The girls, however, have no blood anywhere. Some bruises, indicating something wrapped around their necks, but no blood. It seems these girls were strangled instead of cut.

Wait, one of them has a trace of blood. But the crimson fluid leaked from her nose. The method of killing is very different, although still focused on the neck.

All of them could be classified as redheads, their hair colors ranging from fiery poppy red to deep cabernet, not in that order. So, if they weren't placed in order of hair gradation, then maybe in order of time of death.

Every single one of the girls has a pastel-colored scrunchie on their body. Not always in their hair. Most are around their left wrist, a few are entwined in their hair, and some are positioned under their arms. Pale yellow, robin's egg blue, beige, baby doll pink, even a light celery color. Why? This time period seems older than the 1980s when the hair accessory became popular. Who knew scrunchies were around in the 1970s? Unless I'm wrong about the decade.

I jump as a meaty hand clamps onto my shoulder.

Ranger Rasher's voice is gruff. "I've got the sheriff coming and a highway patrolman."

Oh, great. Another sheriff. After the Shepherd's Town sheriff tried to kill me in 1872, I'd rather not encounter another one. Plus, my stomach won't settle, given the atmosphere. "Can I head back to the cabin?"

Suspicion creeps into Rasher's eyes. I can't blame him. I show up out of nowhere, lead him to some bodies in the forest, and don't want to be around when the cops come. None of that looks good for me. But I can't muster up enough energy to care.

His gaze travels over my shoulder, and his eyes narrow to pinpricks. I spin around to look. Nothing other than trees waving in the slight breeze.

"What is it?" I ask.

He trudges in that direction without a word.

I hesitate for only a second before trailing behind him.

Soon, the trees thin out enough to see a man walking ahead with his back to us. He must have heard our footsteps but doesn't want to talk.

"Gerald, what are you doing here?" Rasher asks in a

demanding, official tone. Perhaps he should have been a police officer.

The man slowly stops, then turns around. It's the same man I saw last night, or more like early this morning—the one without the halo. He wears a fedora-style hat over his bald head. I guess he had more than one hat up here. His brown flannel checked coat is unbuttoned, revealing a grimy yellow cotton shirt underneath.

"Just a little prospecting, Marv." He smirks in my direction. "Who's your friend?"

Rasher folds his arms across his chest. "This is government land. No mines allowed."

The man shrugs. "Perhaps the government will want to sell."

"Not likely."

"Hey, everything is for sale if you have the right connections."

Rasher twists his lips as if the words he wants to say are turning sour in his mouth.

The man shifts his attention back to me. "I'm Gerald Morgan, owner of Sawtooth Creek titanium mine near Hamilton. Are you a prospector too?"

"No."

His eyebrows shoot up, and he nods toward the area behind us—the killing ground. "Just here for recreational activities?"

Is he accusing me of killing these women and girls? Funny how I was just about to insinuate the same thing to him. "Again, no."

"How long have you been prospecting out here, Gerald," Rasher asks.

"A couple of days." His gaze falls to the forest floor. "Not long enough to have seen anything regarding what you just found."

He takes several deep breaths, keeping his gaze downturned. Is he showing respect for the tragedy? Or just hoping we won't see guilt in his eyes?

He flicks a thumb at me. "When I saw you with this guy, I thought you might be showing him some good mining sites. Leaving me out of the loop."

Rasher shakes his head indicating that was a stupid assumption. "He's not a prospector." He takes a backward step toward the crime scene. "Well, if you see anything out here or hear anything in town about this, let me know."

"Will do." Gerald lifts his gaze to stare at me as if daring me to accuse him.

I stare back, matching his aggressive gaze. Perhaps he followed me earlier to see if I was prospecting. Perhaps not. Either way, no halo means he's clearly not the man I saw at the death site.

With a short nod, Rasher turns on his heel and heads back toward the crime scene. I follow once Gerald has returned to his course through the woods.

"I saw him out here last night," I whisper.

"Not surprising. When people prospect, they search during the day and camp at night. When they identify a promising spot, they will often return at night so they can check it out without fear of someone stealing the location."

"Do you think he's looking for titanium?"

A quick shake of his head. "Probably gold. There are a few gold mines south of here." He gives a low growl. "But Gerald won't try to buy the land from the government. He'll just mine what he can in secret."

"Isn't that stealing?"

He gives me a side-eye. "Only if I can catch him."

As we step back into the area of the killing ground, we are both momentarily distracted by Daisy's appearance. She runs straight for a woman, the second down the line, and lets out a few whines. Maybe that's her owner? After a long protracted doggy sigh, she comes over to me and rubs along my leg.

I guess the dog's approval tips Rasher in my favor. "Alright. You can go back to the cabin. Just don't go anywhere else."

That approval is all I need. As the dog and I melt into the forest, Morrow grumbles at Rasher about letting me leave. She's got a point. To her, I look like a good suspect who could disappear and hide any place in this vast wilderness. They would never find me. What they don't know is that they wouldn't have long to find me. Assuming the twenty-one hour return command in my programming still holds, I'll be leaving soon. Maybe even in as little as fifteen hours from now.

Hopefully, I won't encounter Halo Man again in that time. If I keep a low profile, I can just go home and figure out why I'm still leaping into the past without messing anything else up here.

Though the trees now insulate me from the site, the image of those dead girls flashes in my vision. A soft voice tickles the back of my mind. *What if you're not here to mess things up?*

But that would mean I'm here to change things. That I'm *supposed* to change things. Wasn't there an old TV show with such a premise? Oh, yeah, the guy leaped into other people's bodies. Thank God I'm not doing that.

I catch myself. God doesn't have anything to do with this debacle. More than likely, I'm here due to a glitch in my programming. Could have been accidental, but it's probably Akane Souza's fault. And when I get back, she's going to give me some answers.

But then that serene voice tickles my brain again. *What if you're here to save Liam?*

The thought stops my fruitless ruminations. Clearly, my brain has jumped over the edge of a cliff. How am I supposed to save Liam from the wilderness of a time period many decades before he's due to be born?

The trek to the ranger's cabin still takes almost two hours because of the dense trees, even though I now know where I'm going. Daisy bounds ahead and then runs back, all the while looking at me like she's asking what's taking so long.

"I've got two legs, not four, girl."

Finally, the log-cabin-style ranger's station comes into view.

Rasher didn't hand me any keys. This is the middle of nowhere in a more innocent decade, so I'll bet it's unlocked.

Sure enough, the door swings open easily, and Daisy follows me inside. I shut it behind me and peruse the space. A tiny kitchen with a compact refrigerator. One recliner, no TV as Rasher said, and a cot in the corner. A narrow hallway leads to a small bedroom and bathroom in the back. It reminds me of the hunting cabin that Liam took me to in Grand Junction the summer after I met him. We spent a whole weekend fishing and hiking the trails. Liam was also an accomplished hunter, but he didn't hunt that weekend because he knew I couldn't watch him kill animals. Does his family still own that cabin in my home time? Perhaps his parents adopted a different kid who hates being outdoors.

I drop the blanket on the recliner. In the kitchen, I find a thin towel and wrap it around my CRASH device to keep it hidden, tucking the end in on itself. Better than having to make up lies regarding its purpose.

After putting a bowl of water down for Daisy, I stretch out on the cot. She drinks for several minutes, then curls up on the floor in a corner, putting her varicolored tail over her gray nose. If that girl was her owner, where did they come from? A nearby town, maybe Meadowlark, the one Rasher mentioned? Perhaps that's why Daisy sticks around here. Because she failed her owner and doesn't know what to do about it. I can relate to failure, girl.

Even here, I've leaped in too late to help any of those victims. I could try to bring them justice, but maybe my time is better spent trying to bring Liam back, if there's a way to do that here. First, I have to determine what I may have done during my last leap to eliminate him from the future. But how? His birth parents are a mystery he hadn't solved. He was looking for them, and at one point, he told me his birth mother's name, but it didn't stick. I can't remember.

Just as my eyes are drifting closed, I hear a noise outside the window. Slow, halting footsteps. Someone places a palm against the glass with a smack. I startle and sit up. They must be leaning down because I can't see a face.

A female voice lets out a raspy, "Help."

What the heck? I bolt for the door, throw it open, and run around the side of the cabin. A young woman with dark brownish-red hair staggers toward me, wearing underwear and a ripped cotton shirt. But I barely register her state of dress because I'm focused on the blood running down her neck.

"Please, help," she whispers as she collapses against me.

I've seen more gashes and bloody noses than I can count while playing cutthroat basketball and snowmobile hockey, but this woman is severely injured. She might be dying. Did she pass out?

"Miss?"

She comes to with a scream, pushing and scratching me. One of her fingernails nicks the spider bite on my neck that had just started to heal from my last leap. In my dash through the woods last night, I must have lost the bandage covering it. Now we're both bleeding.

"It's okay." I grab her wrists to stop her from struggling. "You're okay."

Daisy whines by my leg. That seems to reorient the woman. She looks up at me with panicked eyes. "You're not him?"

"Not who?"

"Him." She indicates her neck as if saying the man who had done that.

Any fleeting hope this woman had been attacked by an animal is squashed. Certainty settles into my bones. She is the twenty-first victim. Somehow, she's still alive.

For the moment.

"Come inside. You need to lie down."

She leans on me to get through the door, and I direct her to the cot. Once she's lying down, I cover her with the blanket from the recliner, using one corner to stem the bleeding in her neck.

Obviously, her throat hasn't been cut too deep or she'd be dead already.

Even so, she needs immediate medical attention. I take one of her hands and place it on the blanket. "Keep pressure on it."

She grabs my hand, trying to hold on, but her palms are slick with blood. "No, don't leave me."

"I won't. I'm going to call someone. I'll be right back."

There's a phone, but do they have 911 in this time period? Ranger Morrow said there was a radio. After a quick search, I find a two-way radio attached to the side of a cabinet in the kitchen. I've only ever seen one in a museum, but I learned the concept in history class. I depress the lever, which gives me static. Good enough. "Hello?"

"Who is this?" It sounds like Rasher.

"This is Mars. I've got someone here who needs help."

"Say again. Who needs help?"

"A woman. She's bleeding."

I listen to static for a long twenty seconds before he comes back on. "All right. I'm almost to the station. Stay there."

Why would he be almost here? Granted, he can probably hike through the woods faster than I can, but even so, that would mean he'd left shortly after I did.

I return to crouch next to the woman who floats in and out of consciousness. I put pressure on the blanket because she has relaxed her hold. Her eyelids flutter, and she moans. When I take her hand, she flinches.

"Serenity," she says.

We could all use more serenity, but it's an odd thing to say right now.

A weak nod of her head. "My name is Serenity Brooks."

She's probably not joking at a time like this. And such a name would be just the kind of thing to come out of the 1970s, when names like Harmony and Sunshine were popular.

A hissing laugh escapes from her mouth. "I wasn't a serene child. Serves them right."

"Who did this to you?"

A short sigh. "Looked normal … Loved my hair … Said color is like garnet."

Well, her hair is a deep reddish-brown. And unfortunately, most serial killers look normal. This one, apparently, has an obsession with red hair. She lapses into silence again.

Five long minutes later, Rasher bursts in the door with the urgency of a mountain man on a rescue. He joins me at her side, checks under the blanket, and then tugs out his walkie-talkie. "RSD Seven calling Base, come in."

"Base to RSD Seven, go ahead."

"Injured female. Need ambulance to station three. Over."

"Understood. Over."

Silence settles as we wait for help and I continue to put pressure on her neck. Serenity's eyes stay closed, but she's breathing steadily.

"How did you get back so quickly?" I ask. "Didn't you need to help with the scene?"

A shadow flickers across his face. "Lead Ranger Morrow thought I should come check on you. Gave me quite the earful."

So Morrow *is* his boss. I meet his suspicious gaze with what I hope is an innocent expression. "She thinks I had something to do with the killings?"

"What would you think if a strange guy showed up in the middle of nowhere and led you to a dumping ground?" He grunts. "Not to mention finding you here with"—he lowers his voice to a whisper—"a slashed woman."

All good points to which I have no good response.

Rasher continues, "But this isn't all about you."

"What do you mean?"

He purses his lips. "I'll only say Morrow's sister disappeared a while back, and this is likely bringing up the trauma again. She's taking control of the scene, in some way, to take control of her emotions."

Pretty deep for a mountain man. But wait, is he saying …

"No. None of these victims have been out there long enough to be her sister." He peers at me intently. "What's on your neck?"

I put a hand up and fight the urge to scratch the wound. "It's a spider bite. Got infected. She scratched it when I brought her into the cabin."

He narrows his eyes further, then gestures to the blanket. "I'll take over. Go back to my room and get something else to put on."

Of course, my T-shirt is a wreck, smeared with dark crimson blood. This leap has been as detrimental to my clothing as the last one. Rasher is a bit wider than me, but since he's a few inches shorter, I should be able to find something that fits. As I reach the bedroom, I hear sirens in the distance, so I grab the closest shirt I can find and bolt back out.

I throw my soiled shirt into the sink so the blood won't stain anything else. Goodbye, Ms. PacMan. When I look down, my chest has streaks of red across it. I clean up with a damp paper towel and pull on the new T-shirt.

As I take in its design, I glance up at Rasher in surprise. The shirt has several winged people hovering over the caption *Gatchaman*. Who knew this was a thing in the 1970s? "Anime?"

Rasher shrugs. "I spent last summer in Japan. That series isn't available in the US." He scowls. "Be careful with that shirt."

I give him a small salute.

The paramedics burst through the door without bothering to knock, hauling a stretcher between them. It's about time. It seemed like I could hear their sirens forever. But long distances seem to be a feature of whatever part of the country I'm in.

Both of the paramedics are men. The first one in the door checks below the blanket, then nods to his partner. They begin to load her onto the stretcher—the first man grabbing her feet, the other beneath her shoulders.

The movement rouses her. Her eyes fly open, but apparently, she can't keep them open. After her eyes close again, she mumbles something that sounds like "Pep."

It doesn't mean anything to me. Rasher seems just as dumb-founded. Maybe she was trying to say, "Please help me"?

He grabs his walkie-talkie again, presumably to tell Ranger Morrow about the development. I go to the window and watch the ambulance leave.

What if Serenity is the reason I came to this time period? To save her. That would be worth the detour.

My heart does a little jump. Maybe she's Liam's birth mother. It's possible, but I rein in my hope. There's no way for me to know. How am I supposed to make him a priority when I don't have any idea who is related to him?

No matter what, saving Serenity would at least make this experience meaningful. So would stopping a serial killer. The image of all those women and girls lined up streaks through my mind again, dissecting my thoughts like a knife blade. Did I show up in time to prevent the twenty-first victim? Or will she fill that role, despite my efforts?

CHAPTER 4

THE MACHINES at Serenity's bedside in the hospital beep with the rhythm of her soft snores. A bandage snakes around her neck, concealing the killer's mark. The doctors won't make any guarantees, but they seem to think she'll survive. Did my intervention save her, or would she have made it in the previous timeline anyway? I'll never know the answer.

I'm trying to make sense of these leaps in time. To make a difference when I'm here, but I don't even know *why* I'm here specifically. Is this another intersection of Millstone and Lockporte DNA like my first leap? Or is this leap solely about Liam? Or could both be true?

I need to ask more questions, but it's a bit suspicious to start asking everyone if they're related to me or to someone from the future.

In 2051, Seth Millstone killed my best friend and basketball teammate, Kiefer Deglan, spurring my initial leap into the past. That first leap eliminated Seth from the future—thus saving Kiefer—but it also eliminated Liam, the third friend in our basketball trio. Could it be that the fates of Seth Millstone and Liam Crosby are intertwined? To save one is to save the other, leaving Kiefer always at risk?

Nothing profound comes to mind to answer any of these questions. I go back to the basic facts: Liam must have been related to one of the people who died in my last leap, either Sheriff Dillard or the Millstone brothers. If he's a Millstone, then I've got no chance to change anything in this time period since I ended that family line. Maybe he was related to Sheriff Dillard, then?

I shake my head to shake off the generational rabbit hole I'm tumbling down. Changing the future is too much responsibility. Perhaps I saved Serenity. Or perhaps she'll die despite the doctors' assurances. Would one way be for the greater good? For all I know, Serenity's descendants might create a new kind of weapon or lead a mass genocide.

Swiping a hand through my hair, I blow out a breath to bring me back from the ledge. The last time I saved someone, Long Browning, his descendant became our new president, one who seems to fairly represent the people. I have to believe the best about Serenity and anyone who is descended from her.

A wet nose nudges my hand, grounding me in the moment again. Daisy had jumped in Rasher's truck as soon as we opened the door, determined not to be left behind. I snuck her in here because I didn't want her to run off again. Now, she whines for some unknown reason. Maybe she's hungry or needs to go out. I have no food, but I can take her outside.

As I stand, a new nurse enters to check Serenity's vitals. She goes to the other side of the bed, so she doesn't see Daisy. The woman is probably around thirty, and like all the others, she's wearing the epitome of a vintage nursing outfit with a white knee-length utilitarian dress, white rubber-soled shoes, and a pointy paper cap pinned in her curly strawberry-blond hair. She gives me an encouraging smile. "Your sweetheart is doing well. The accident shouldn't affect her at all once she heals."

I stiffen. Not because she assumes Serenity is my girlfriend, but because she said "accident." The rangers obviously haven't told the staff that Serenity is a crime victim.

"She's not my girlfriend. I was just trying to help her. Her family probably misses her."

The police must want to keep the investigation quiet, but is that possible in a small town like this? When I rode with Rasher to the hospital, I saw the entire area is made up of mountains and trees. This small town virtually appeared in a large divot in the landscape as if the mountains funneled all the people to the low point like water heading down a drain.

So, I could be in any of the colder mountainous states: Colorado, Idaho, Montana, Washington, even parts of Wyoming have mountain ranges. One sure clue is that I'm in the Ravalli County Hospital. Such a great help.

Nothing in this room has been able to give me an address either. All the magazines are without labels. The hospital food menu only lists the hospital's name. And there's not even a TV for me to try to find the local news.

At least the magazines tell me I'm pretty close on the date. The most recent one is from June 1972.

"Are you injured?" The nurse comes around the bed toward me while pointing at my towel-wrapped elbow.

"No. Just a scratch. It's fine."

"Oh, sweet baby," the nurse croons to Daisy. "I didn't see you sitting so nicely there."

The dog sits taller as if to say, *See, someone appreciates me.*

"But you're not supposed to be in here." The nurse looks over her shoulder as if some administrator will come kick us out.

Maybe they will.

"What's her name?"

I rub my neck and wince as I touch the spider bite. "We've been calling her Daisy, but she's not my dog."

She gestures to Serenity. "Her dog?"

"Not sure. I found the dog just before finding her. I couldn't let it wander in the woods alone."

"I see." Her tone and demeanor soften, and her eyebrows arch with interest.

Uh-oh. I've gone from unavailable boyfriend to rescuing, dog-loving hero. Maybe if she knew about the body dumping ground a few miles away, she'd be more cautious with a stranger, even one claiming to be a rescuer.

She takes a step toward me and sways her hips a bit. Some of her curls have been left in front of her hat to frame her smooth pale face. She's a lovely girl, but not my type. Even if she were, I've got another girl stuck in my head right now, one who also loves animals.

"Um." I squint at her nametag. "Nurse Gammon—"

"Call me Ivory." She takes another slow step toward me. "The patient is sedated and should be unconscious for several more hours."

I take a step away from her.

"I have a break coming up."

Whoa. She's misreading all my signals.

"I don't want you and the dog to be forced to leave. Would you like someplace to keep her? My standard poodle would love a playmate for the day."

I blink at her. That is not the direction I thought she was headed. But actually … "Nurse Gammon, I'm sure Daisy would love that."

"Great. And it's Ivory. My house is just a short walk down Bedford Street." She checks Serenity's monitors one more time before saying, "Ms. Brooks should be fine while we're gone, but Nurse Hughes will watch my patients during my break."

As we leave via the front entrance, Ivory and I chat about the town. When I came with Rasher, we entered the hospital from the back, which seemed to be an alleyway with no street sign at all. The front entrance, in contrast, is a grand portico with four Grecian columns and wide stairs leading to the sidewalk. Fancy for a hospital.

On the walk to her residence, which turns out to be a cute white ranch house with a cottage-style arched entrance, I switch the subject to ask about her strangest nursing case. She tells me of a man who came to the hospital with abdominal pains after swallowing a tortoise as a consequence of losing a drinking game. Amazingly, doctors removed the tortoise unharmed hours later.

"Afterward, he reportedly couldn't be near a live tortoise without sweating profusely and panicking." She laughs. "Serves him right."

"I agree."

From behind her front door, her poodle barks in staccato at us. In a quick motion, Ivory upends a garden gnome and digs a key from under its feet. Not the most secure hiding place, but at least she locks her door. Probably a fair amount of people in this small town don't.

"Thanks for letting her play with your dog," I say.

"Of course. Any guy who cares about animals is a good guy, right?"

I nod, though her logic is faulty in the extreme. In the future, I've heard of serial killers who adore their pets and yet continue to murder people.

We let Daisy in to meet Baxter, the tall poodle, and they get along wonderfully. Ivory pulls some more toys from a basket and lays them on the floor, along with some food. Daisy goes straight for the food, gobbling it up in seconds.

"You know, Daisy looks familiar."

"How so?"

Ivory taps her finger on her bottom lip. "I think she came in a month or so ago with a woman who was treated for dehydration. The woman wasn't my patient, but I tend to remember animals."

"What happened to the woman?"

"She recovered. After a couple of hours on an IV drip, she felt better and checked herself out. I never saw her again."

So if Daisy belongs to that woman who then ended up becoming a victim, it would explain why the dog was running around in the woods alone. I could ask Ivory for the woman's name, but it won't help much until the police identify the victims, and it might be a while before they do. I'll let Rasher know. The police can search the hospital records later.

Ivory moves toward the front door. "These two should be fine. Baxter loves other dogs."

After a quick rubdown for both Daisy and Baxter, who trotted over so as not to be left out, I follow Ivory to the front yard.

As she closes and locks the door, she gives me a wink. "Baxter seemed to like you too."

I merely smile. I've always had a way with animals. More than likely, they can sense that I'm a critter lover.

Ivory doesn't seem to mind my questions, so on the way back, I ask general info about the residents of the town. Nothing interesting comes out of my gentle interrogation. At the massive steps to the hospital, she asks if I'd like to get some food with her to finish out her break. As enticing as food sounds, I have other plans. The scientist in me knows it's time for research.

"I appreciate the offer, but I've got something I need to look into. Can you point me in the direction of the library?"

CHAPTER 5

Turns out the library is situated just one block up on the corner of Fourth Street and State Street. Ivory doesn't understand why I need to do research at this moment, but she doesn't need to. I simply tell her I won't be long and head north.

As I work my way past the front of the hospital, down Fourth Street, the long line of trees on both sides of the lane reminds me of the victims, their bodies stretched out in two perfect rows. They didn't get the chance to visit a hospital. They had no one to rescue them. They died staring not at a quaint street but at the face of their killer.

Hopefully, Serenity will give the police a lead when she wakes up. A flush of guilt rushes over me for not sitting by her bedside. But that's stupid. If she wakes while I'm gone, the nurses will take care of her. I barely know her and have no official ties to her.

Same with Rasher, who went back to the forest an hour ago after a quick check on Serenity's status. He and Morrow are helping the state police investigate the large crime scene. Perhaps this is taking too high a toll on Morrow. Rasher didn't say how old her sister was when she disappeared or how old

Morrow was, for that matter. But deep wounds never really heal; they just develop ugly scars.

Back to the problems at hand—where am I and what year am I in? My sister, Gaia, is a big crime junkie, so I rack my brain trying to remember if she mentioned a case in the early 1970s with this many bodies. But my mind is a blank. Even throwing in all the possible mountainous states doesn't help jog my memory.

The air is calm and crisp, certainly above sixty degrees now. It must be getting close to noon, promising warmer temperatures for the rest of the day. The fresh air revives my spirit. I can handle this leap. I just need more information.

Sure enough, State Street is the next crossroad. At the northeast corner sits a building with a sign labeled Bitterroot Public Library. I assume I'm in Meadowlark since Rasher mentioned the town name earlier. He also said we were in the Bitterroot National Forest, so the surrounding mountains are most likely the Bitterroot Mountain Range. I think that's in the western part of the country? Or is that the Bighorn Mountain range?

The small brick building is barely big enough to be a house, much less a community library. Inside, the atmosphere is homey, and the smell of books makes me nostalgic. In my town in 2051, books are outlawed. Not because of some censorship craze but because of environmental concerns. Killing a tree to read a book is self-indulgent and irresponsible. Only the authors themselves are allowed to have one copy that can be passed down through the family line, which is how I have a copy of my father's book at home. The reason why I keep it would be a question for a seasoned family therapist. The book is an elaborate story of my battle with early onset dementia—a disease I never had—and the cure my dad purported to have. He used me, my sister, and my mother to generate cash in any way he could. Not for us but for him. Thus, I come by my distrust of people naturally.

Speaking of my mother, the middle-aged librarian looks a bit like her. That is, if Mom had worn a dress past her knees and a gaudy gold pin—maybe they call them broaches?—shaped like a starburst. Her taupe-colored hair is tied back in a loose bun, and her small features give her a delicate appearance, but her violet eyes are bright and curious.

"Can I help you, young man?" She looks quizzically at the towel in the crook of my arm but doesn't ask.

A bout of homesickness rolls over me at her motherly tone. Her voice is nothing like Mom's, but I could sure use someone to talk to. Jumping around in time is disconcerting enough, especially when I can't be sure I'll make it back home. Perhaps this time I've sent myself into a recurring loop, leaping from time to time without end.

I swallow down my doomsday thoughts and smile. What *am* I looking for? Maybe if I learn more about the families in this town, I'll have a better idea of why I leaped here.

"Hello, ma'am. I'm new in town and wanted to look up some local history."

"Oh, my. I didn't realize we had a new resident. I would have sent the welcome wagon ladies to your door. Where did you move in?"

I shake my head. "Sorry for the confusion. I haven't moved in. I'm just looking at the community as a possibility for a move."

"A visitor, then. We get lots of people looking to enjoy the sky around here." She winks.

Not sure what that means. Thankfully, I don't have to respond. She gets busy handing me brochures. Before I can look at them, she waves me over to a corner table. "Sit here. To know a place, you have to know its history. I'm going to bring you our most prized historical book. You can't check it out, though. Have to read it here. It seems like you have a little time?"

I nod, so she hustles toward a bookshelf behind an ornate desk.

Which brochure to look at first? I fan them out, and one catches my eye. *Meadowlark, Gateway to Montana's Bitterroot Mountains.* Two more flyers mention the state.

Then, I find the brochure for the library. The address on the bottom is 306 State Street, Meadowlark, Montana. Of course, it makes sense now. Montana's nickname is Big Sky Country.

So, I'm in the small community of Meadowlark with no transportation, nestled in the remote wilderness of the Bitterroot Mountains near a serial killer's body farm. A total setup for a horror film. But I can't just run around blindly hoping I don't run into the killer. Time to stop wishing I was back home and start figuring out what's going on here. To determine if there's a reason I'm in this time and place.

The librarian returns with a thick volume and thunks it on the table. Frayed edges stick out on all sides. She throws the book open to a random page.

Suddenly, she pats her heart. "Oh, my memory. There's a listing of documents."

"Thank you, ma'am."

"Call me Mrs. Keller." She throws the words over her shoulder as she rummages in a desk drawer.

In the meantime, I glance at the fragile paper in front of me. It's a bill of sale for some horses sold by Nelson Price, dated June 17, 1872. Really old stuff. The next page lists stock for a business, probably a grocery store based on the itemized fresh fruit.

"Here it is." Mrs. Keller places a typed sheet on the table next to me, but she doesn't sit. "I have some inventory to finish in the kids' section."

I had missed the tote of children's books sitting on the floor on the other side of the room.

"Let me know if you need anything else or if this isn't the kind of documents you'd like to read."

"Thank you, Mrs. Keller. I appreciate it."

It has been a long time since I've touched a book other than my father's, but I've never touched historical documents before. I run my fingers along the paper again, savoring the fine texture marred sporadically by wrinkles, like scars on smooth skin testifying to the hardships endured on a difficult journey.

I flip a page to find a deed executed by two people with the last name Jenkins. I scan through the next several pages without discovering anything familiar or helpful. Now that the historical awe is wearing off, this exercise seems daunting.

The list of documents calls to me as a way to scan through things faster. I push the book away and drag the paper closer. The typewritten words slant down to the left as if someone had placed it in the typewriter at an angle.

Column headings are listed across the top: Date, Name, Family Surname, Type of Document, and Location. The Location column has a page number corresponding to a small, typed sticker placed on the bottom of the pages. The dates range from 1862 to 1917. Mrs. Keller must have picked the first historical book she had since many of the western states weren't settled until the 1880s or later.

I peruse the Family Surname column. Three-quarters of the way down the page, I gasp.

"Everything okay, Mr. ...?"

I clear my throat. "Lockporte, ma'am. I'm fine. Just surprised that some of these names seem familiar because I'm not from around here."

"Odd for you to say that. Lockporte sounds vaguely familiar to me too." She shrugs and goes back to checking books off her list.

I lock my gaze onto the entry that shouldn't be a shock to me by this point. The listed surname associated with an enclosed frontier diary is Millstone. A letter written by Ava Millstone is located on page 86.

I flip to that page. It's a letter dated April 16, 1872, written in a rushed but pretty, rolling script. Surely, this woman isn't related to the Millstones who died because of my intervention in the Civil War. That was in West Virginia, nowhere close to Montana.

One scan of the first line tells me how wrong my assumption is.

CHAPTER 6

April 16, 1872

Dearest Mother,

If I could write a hundred apology letters to you, it would not be enough to atone for the unforgivable way I left the comfort of your presence when I abandoned our home near Shepherd's Town in West Virginia. What kind of wretched daughter leaves without a word? Please know my actions had nothing to do with abandoning you, though I realize I have done so.

Our separation until my sixteenth year put me in the care of Herman Johnson, where you found me, this much you have known. However, I have not relayed to you the entirety of the circumstances that drove me to Mr. Johnson's home.

After my birth, your midwife, Prisca, placed me in the care of a young couple, the Fowlers, who had been waiting several years for a child. They treated me as a cherished daughter always. I spent twelve happy years there as they added a brother and sister to the brood. One afternoon, a man visited the homestead claiming to be my father. I knew nothing of him—or you—

so Mr. Fowler would not let me depart with him. The man struck Mr. Fowler beyond consciousness and spirited me away despite Mrs. Fowler's protests.

This unknown man and I moved from place to place for several months, barely surviving. The Fowlers contacted Prisca, who confirmed the parentage of my natural father. Much later, I heard such from Prisca, but I had already knit the information together into an understandable reality. This man had somehow availed himself of you. Your husband did not wish to raise another man's child, thus I was sent away. I harbor no blame for these decisions made on my behalf since I have no claim to know what path I would choose in such a conundrum.

Reginald—the man gave me this moniker as his name, which I now know to be false—had not touched me, even though I could sense his lusting. He bade me to sleep with my back to his front and his arms curled around me at night.

For weeks, I dallied with thoughts of Mr. Fowler coming to rescue me. After many more weeks, it was not Mr. Fowler but Prisca who appeared, though I did not know her as yet. She had trailed us to an old barn. We were burning pieces of the walls for warmth as the October night had grown cool.

While I squatted in the corner, a place I used as the necessary since he would not allow me to venture out, I heard a veiled whisper. An almond-shaped eye peered at me through a knot in a board.

I swallowed down my yelp fast enough to hear a soft voice say, "Friend."

I hesitated but a moment before I nodded. Perhaps she could help me escape.

The woman passed a small vial to me via the knothole. "Put this in his water to induce sleep."

Not daring to speak in answer, I nodded again as I hid the vial in my skirts.

"Girl, what are you doing over there? The fire needs tending."

"Of course. May I have a drink first?"

A grunt was his only response, affirmation enough for me. I bent over at the waist and daintily picked up the ladle from our water bucket with my right hand. I sipped while unsealing the cap on the vial with my left hand, doing this under the concealment of the folds of my skirt. The moment he looked away, I dumped the white powder into the ladle and dropped it back in the bucket. It may have been too great an amount to use the entirety of the container. The water bucket was merely half full, after all. Yet, I was not so very concerned with his welfare at the time.

I tended the fire with my stomach growling from hollowness while roasting a few mushrooms he had found under a nearby tree. Before I could pilfer a bite, he absconded with the stick and sucked the charred delicacies down in one swallow.

Fortune favored me when the mushrooms made him thirsty. He lifted the bucket by both sides and drank deeply. After wiping his mouth with his shirtsleeve, he retreated to the side wall of the barn and sank to the ground with a satisfied look on his face.

Within moments, the satisfied look morphed into a veneer of panic. He leaned to the side and vomited in the dirt. Bits of mushroom spewed out in every direction. Had he regurgitated the full measure of powder? Perhaps I had wasted the entirety of the vial for no result. I should have been more cautious and not fully entertained my desperation for escape.

His head dropped backward against the barn wall with a thunk. My breath caught in my throat. His eyes were open, but his breathing seemed to slow. Or did I imagine the shallowness of breath?

When he closed his eyes, I dared to hope the powder would do its job. I took a step toward him. He raised his lids as if creaking open a rusty door. Then, they fell back closed.

Next, I truly heard a rusty door opening, and Prisca stepped into the barn. She introduced herself as I enveloped her in a spontaneous embrace.

When I pulled away, I wiped a tear from the corner of my eye. "I fear I have inadvertently killed him."

Prisca smiled in sympathy. "No, dear one. He slumbers. In point of fact, you likely saved his life. Those mushrooms are full of poison. The extra dose of sleeping powder forced him to expel what may have killed him."

Relief flooded over me. I was not a murderess.

At her direction, we vacated the barn and escaped into the woods.

"Please return me home," I said as Prisca began following a clear heading.

She did not turn around. "Alas, I cannot fulfill your request. Your previous home would be the primary spot for your father to search for you. Doing such would put the Fowlers in danger."

From a young age, the Fowlers had informed me of my status as an adopted daughter, but I had never asked about my natural parents. Since Mr. and Mrs. Fowler raised me, that had been parenting enough for me. I wished to return to the only parents I knew. Yet, Prisca made a convincing argument. I cared for them enough to keep them safe. "Where, then?"

"To a man whose daughter succumbed to consumption several years ago."

Along the way, we spoke of you and your two grown sons, though she never confessed your name, nor the true name of my father whom we had left in the barn.

Eventually, she delivered me to Herman Johnson, who also treated me like a true daughter. God had been preparing the way for our mother-daughter reunion even then. Herman loosened his tongue one night after several glasses of heavy mead and admitted he knew the identity of my mother, a Millstone. Thus, I added your name as my surname to become Ava Fowler Millstone. He could not tell me if you gave me the name Ava, but I always believed you did.

A month after my sixteenth birthday, just as I was considering how to begin the search for you, you appeared on our front portico. Even before you spoke, I suspected your identity from your unique rosy shade of hair, like the yellowish-red glow of a sunset scattered on storm clouds. That is how Herman once described my hair coloring.

When you relayed what had caused you to search for me, my heart broke for you. Such loss you have endured. After we found each other, remember how I wept with you many nights in your grief? You never expected me to replace your beloved Carlton and Francis, taken by the vicious War of the States, and yet I tried to ease your loneliness.

If only I could have stayed with you far longer. Two years was not nearly long enough to compensate for the years we lost.

My father—Edwin Moore, as you told me—found me in Shephard's Town as I was leaving the apothecary's store one afternoon. Since I had more errands to complete, I had just requested to have the clerk deliver the tincture to help your joint pain.

"Alma, here you are." He grabbed my arm and insisted I leave with him at once. It did not register in his mind how he'd called me by your given name, not my own.

To my good fortune, Robert Newman happened to be strolling the street at this very moment. Given his romantic interest in me, Robert approached, and he instantly realized the graveness of the situation.

"Take your hand from her," he demanded.

My father obeyed without looking at Robert. He focused solely on me as he said, "If you do not go with me willingly, I will force you."

"You will not, sir," Robert declared. "I will ensure the safety of this woman."

If only I could believe it to be true. Edwin Moore had shown he would stop at nothing to have me with him. And the slip in nomenclature confirmed I had completely supplanted you in his mind. His obsession was mine alone to bear. He would follow after me if I left. Thus, you would only be in danger if I stayed.

My father finally looked at Robert and retreated. "This is not the end."

"It must be," Robert replied with a narrowing of his eyes. "You will leave this woman in peace."

My father had already turned his back to stride away and gave no reply.

I placed a hand on Robert's cheek. "Thank you. I regret that I must go."

Robert would have thought I meant to return home. He could not imagine I would disappear from his life permanently. Yet, my thoughts were not of him and the life we could have had together. No, my heart hung heavy in my chest because I had to leave you.

I can only imagine how you have grieved in the last eight years for another child lost to you. Please understand the difficulty and my own grief caused by the decision I was forced to make.

I traveled as far as I could while taking sustenance from the land and avoiding people altogether, eventually finding myself in the Montana Territory, hungry and filthy.

A dark-skinned woman from one of the earth-living tribes found me and gave me food. We could not speak to each other, but she took care of me like another mother. For several months, I stayed with her and her child in a teepee. Her name was Elu. When the men looked at me with suspicion, she shooed them away. I lived with her peacefully ... excepting the horrific events of one bloody night.

Many of the men had gone off to hunt in far lands. We slept peacefully until the first gunshot cracked through the air. Elu took hold of her small child and wanted to run out, but I halted her. We needed to determine what we were running toward. I peered out the opening of the teepee to see pale-skinned men in military uniforms traversing from tent to tent, shooting all those contained inside.

Almost at once, the flap to our teepee was thrown back. We were confronted by a soldier wielding a gun. His eyes went wide at the sight of me with my pale skin, then he turned his gun on Elu as her child cowered behind her.

Immediately, I stepped in front of Elu, placing my body between her and the weapon. The soldier hesitated. As I suspected, it was not so easy a feat to shoot a white woman.

I spoke to him in a gentle tone. "She is simply a young mother who has helped a stranger in need. Spare her, if you please."

The soldier furrowed his brow for a brief time. Then, he backed out of the opening. I gathered Elu and her child behind me. Her tent was situated at the edge of the clearing, thus we darted toward the surrounding woods amid the din of screams and the crackling of fire.

If I think on it too long, I can still conjure up the sickly smell. The soldiers were burning the tents with the wounded still inside.

My heart filled with anger and sorrow. Regretfully, I could not save all, only these two.

We traveled deeper into the Montana Territory to avoid nearby settlements and to rejoin those of her people who were left. I was content to continue living with them, certainly a place where my father would never look. However, I soon met a fur trader from the Idaho Territory named Monroe whose compassion and kindness toward the natives stirred my soul.

I have since married said fur trader, though I will never change my surname from Millstone, as a reminder of what I had to leave behind and as a way to honor you for as long as I live.

Forgive me for waiting so long to send this missive. I feared my father would continue to watch you to discover clues to my whereabouts. I could not risk having him find me or my sweet young child. Please respond and send your letter to the area of Salmon City in the Idaho Territory to let me know of your well-being.

In all sincerest love,
Ava Fowler Millstone

CHAPTER 7

My mouth has dropped open, and I suck in a sharp breath. Thankfully, Mrs. Keller is still busy with her books, so she doesn't notice. So many thoughts run spastically through my brain that I might be having a seizure. Finally, my gray matter latches on to a quote from Mother Teresa that has been buried deep in my mind:

I alone cannot change the world, but I can cast a stone across the waters to create many ripples.

Time travel creates ripples that build upon each other until a tsunami crashes into the established timeline. My actions killed Carlton and Francis, ending the Millstone family line … or so I thought.

Francis and Carlton had a half sister they knew nothing about. But why is this letter here and not in West Virginia? Either Ava didn't send it, or her descendants returned it to the general area where she had lived. Hopefully, it's the latter. It seems too cruel for Mrs. Millstone to have died not knowing what happened to Ava.

Somehow, Ava found her way to Idaho, close to Montana,

about a hundred years before I leaped here. That can't be a coincidence. Could Liam have been a part of Ava Millstone's family line? But if I fix things so that Liam will exist in the future, does that mean Seth Millstone—the guy who killed my other friend—will come back? I have to take the chance. I refuse to accept that I must choose between Kiefer and Liam.

The library phone rings, and Mrs. Keller rushes to answer.

The document feels fragile between my fingers. There must be more to Ava's story as it played out in this area. I flip back to the list of documents. An asterisk marks the end of her listing, along with several others. Another asterisk at the bottom notates *Further Documents Bound in Book M of Frontier Diaries.*

There must be more. I have to read the rest, but first, I need a record of this part. While Mrs. Keller is distracted, I slip my phone from my back pocket. It opens onto the genealogy quarto that houses my family research. When storage was much more limited, all data on phones used to be housed within an app, which often had to be connected to the internet to function. With the proliferation of AI, devices now have quartos in addition to apps, named for an old style of printing in which they used two regular-sized sheets of paper to make a small folded book with eight pages. But a quarto can hold more like the equivalent of millions of pages within a few megabytes of data.

I swipe my research into the background and snap quick pictures of the pages. Then, I rush to where she had gotten the volume of letters from. After locating Book M and finding one subsequent entry, I check for her signature on the bottom. Yep, this completes the set of Ava's letters.

Mrs. Keller's side of the conversation filters into my ears as I hide my phone in the crook of my arm and take a photo of each page. "Oh, my. Poor thing."

As I snap the last one, I look up to see her nodding her head … at me.

"Yes, he's right here." She holds the phone receiver out to me. "It's the hospital."

Using my elbow, I capture my phone and glue it tight to my side, out of sight. Only the nurse knew I would be here. I hustle over and take the phone, dropping my own phone in my back pocket as I do so. "Hello?"

"Mr. Lockporte, this is Nurse Ivory Gammon from the hospital." Her tone is much more official than when I saw her an hour earlier.

"Call me Mars. What's going on?"

Her tone softens. "Mars, the patient you were observing has taken a turn for the worse. She's gone into a coma and may not survive another hour. I thought you'd want to know."

"Yes. I'll be right there."

After thanking Mrs. Keller for her help, I rush out and jog to the hospital. Less than ten minutes have elapsed, but when I walk in, I don't see Ivory anywhere. A slender, middle-aged nurse glances at me but doesn't react as I stride past her toward Serenity's room. Ivory isn't in there either. Serenity lies on her back in bed. Alone.

I shake her arm gently, but she doesn't wake.

A different young nurse, this one a blonde with her hair curled in a flip at the ends, enters the room holding a pillow. She startles when she sees me. "Friend or family?"

"Friend. Nurse Gammon just called me. What happened?"

"We aren't sure. Her organs are shutting down. We don't have an answer for why." A sad shake of her head. "She's so young too."

"Does that mean she's not going to make it?"

"The odds are against her waking up. But the next couple of hours will be crucial." She places the pillow behind Serenity's head. "Sit with her. Talk to her. It might help."

Well, I could use someone to talk to who won't judge what I'm going through or have me involuntarily committed for saying insane things. After the nurse leaves, I lower myself into the chair next to Serenity and, in a quiet voice, pour out my story. She won't likely remember it if she wakes up, and even if she does, I'll pass it off as a strange dream she had. Telling the tale relieves a weight like a pack of mules from my shoulders and helps me make sense of the chaos in my head, but of course, Serenity doesn't give me any answers to my dilemma, not even an eyelid flutter.

Her expression is peaceful and placid. Will she recover? Or will she slip into oblivion on a whisper of breath? She has a hometown somewhere. Someone must be missing her. She probably has dreams to fulfill, but instead she lies in a hospital bed fighting for her life. Did I leap here just to watch her die? To witness her becoming the twenty-first victim? If only I could have gotten her help sooner.

"I'm sorry," I whisper.

I take her hand and draw it toward me. Something slides from beneath her forearm. A cylinder of plastic. No, a syringe. I roll it through my fingers. That shouldn't be *under* her arm. Like it was hidden there. A small amount of liquid is still in the top of the barrel.

I'm about to call for the nurse when an alarm blares on the machine next to Serenity's bed. She's in distress. My stomach drops to my toes as a gruesome possibility pummels me. She may have been poisoned. But by whom?

The middle-aged nurse rushes into the room, followed by the young nurse and several men dressed in scrubs. Where is Ivory?

While the others edge me out of the way to help Serenity, the middle-aged nurse—Nurse Hughes, according to her name tag —zeroes in on me, specifically my hand holding the syringe.

"What did you do?" she demands.

I frantically shake my head. "Nothing. This was under her arm. I found it right before she—"

My explanation is cut off by Nurse Hughes literally grabbing me by the top portion of my left ear. *Dang!* That hurts.

She drags me from the room, and I nearly drop the syringe. But it's evidence, so I clamp my fingers around it. Granted, I've contaminated it with my fingerprints, but this may be the best lead regarding what is happening to Serenity.

In the hallway, Nurse Hughes uses my momentum from my struggling to throw me into the hallway wall. Seems she's done this a time or two.

"Did you kill that poor girl?" she asks.

"No." I swallow hard. "Of course not."

She glares at me, her nose six inches from mine because I'm slumped against the wall. It would be an effective intimidation tactic for most people, but I've been in this position many times before. Not under the scrutiny of my mother, who seemed to know what I was doing without having to interrogate me, but under the scrutiny of my sister. Gaia could demand information and inflict small amounts of pain at the same time—a tweak of the nose, a twist of a finger, even a pinch to the notoriously sensitive area behind the ear. I don't break easily. Except this time, I haven't done anything to deserve it.

"I wasn't here when she went into the coma. Nurse Gammon called me at the library. Ask the librarian."

"You can be sure I will do just that."

Another nurse rushes over, who looks barely old enough to be an adult. "Have you seen Nurse Gammon?" she asks.

I slide out from under Nurse Hughes's glare and point at the girl. "Good question, where is she?"

"I had to help one of her patients because she never came back after checking him in," the nurse says. "I verified in the schedule book. Her shift doesn't end for four more hours."

I blurt out, "Maybe she used the syringe on Serenity and left to escape capture?"

Throwing Ivory under the bus like this doesn't sit right with me, but it's a possibility. She didn't seem like the type to poison an innocent woman. Although, murderers don't wear name tags identifying them as disturbed serial killers.

One of the men in scrubs walks out of Serenity's room while

shaking his head. We all fixate on him. He gives Nurse Hughes a somber look that can only mean one thing.

Serenity is dead.

Nurse Hughes turns to me, but I shove the syringe in her face. "You need to analyze what's in this and determine whether Nurse Gammon would have access to it."

Nurse Hughes must agree with my internal assessment of Ivory's innocence because she aims another scalding glare at me as if she can't believe my impudence. She has no idea how impudent I can be. Or how persistent. Serenity was so close to surviving her ordeal and returning to whatever family she has. If I couldn't save her during my time here, then I will figure out who did this to her.

CHAPTER 8

Nurse Hughes instructs me to sit until the police arrive. While she calls the librarian to check my alibi, I fidget on a row of connected plastic bucket chairs. This is all wrong.

Why would Ivory call me back to the hospital if she intended to leave? Just to pin the murder on me? A murder that had already happened during the time I was at the library. It doesn't make sense.

Another possibility rears its ugly head. Perhaps she saw the person who poisoned Serenity. What if Ivory has been taken by that person? But if so, why wouldn't they have taken her right away? How did she have time to call me? The only answer that comes to mind is she must not have immediately realized what the person had done. Perhaps because this is someone she trusts.

Down the hall, a familiar brown flannel coat catches my eye. What is Gerald Morgan doing here?

As if he can feel me looking at him, he stops talking to a nurse and glances my way. He seems to size me up, though his conclusion is impossible to decipher. The nurse hands him a prescription bottle, which grabs his attention again. After a few more words exchanged with her, he moves down the hall in my direction. I remain seated.

His coat is draped over his shoulders, but only his left arm is inside it. His right forearm is covered in bandages.

"What happened?" I ask.

"A friendly coon. I found what I thought was a small cave. Apparently, I disturbed his nap in his burrow."

A raccoon? Maybe. Or is he covering up another type of animal bite? One he received a while ago when Daisy fought for her owner's life? When I saw him in the woods, he had the coat on, which would have hidden any injuries.

He scratches the stubble on his jaw. "Why are you here?"

He stole my next question. Unfortunately, I don't have a good answer. Telling him about Serenity might compromise the investigation, especially if he's somehow involved. Better to ask another question of my own. "Do you know Nurse Ivory Gammon?"

He tilts his head and peers at me, as if I'm a six-foot-three Jenga puzzle. Like he's wondering which piece he can pull out to get the whole thing to fall apart. "No. I don't know her. Should I?"

"Probably not."

I hang my head to stare between my feet as a way of dismissing him. It's not like he would tell me if he'd taken Ivory. His presence here is disconcerting, though. Gerald takes the hint and leaves.

With my gaze focused on the dirty linoleum floor, I continue to flip through the limited possibilities of people I've met who could have taken Ivory. Maybe Halo Man. Or maybe someone I haven't met. Ivory would know many more people in this town than I do. I don't have enough information to figure this out.

A shadow darkens the space between my feet. I look up to see Rasher's frowning face.

"Can't stay out of trouble, can you?"

I give a humorless laugh. "Not for lack of trying. Did they call you to come get me?"

"Nah. I needed get more supplies."

He holds out a folded medical bag. The end part of a plunger from a syringe pokes out the front.

I try to keep my voice steady as I ask, "What are those for?"

"Diabetes. I have to inject myself with two types of insulin every day. I thought I had more, but when I got back to the ranger's station, I realized I had only two vials."

Chills wash down my spine. An overdose of insulin could certainly put someone in a coma. Possibly kill them. Could Rasher be the killer? With what motive? I suppose he could be secretly in love with Lead Ranger Brenda Morrow, so he kills women and girls who have red hair like her. But it doesn't fit. I didn't see any hint of attraction between those two.

Plus, Rasher isn't likely to be the killer because he isn't Halo Man. Unless Halo Man was at the kill site innocently like me.

No way. Halo Man tried to kill me. He's not innocent.

I rub my temples to dispel the headache forming there. No matter what rabbit trail I go down, nothing makes sense.

This all must lead back to Halo Man. What if he came here to finish off Serenity? He could have injected her, been interrupted by Ivory, and hidden the syringe. At that point, he would know Ivory is a liability. An autopsy would eventually confirm the cause of death, and then Ivory would implicate him. So, he waits for an opportunity and takes her sometime after she calls me. That seems a likelier scenario.

"She's one of my best employees," Nurse Hughes says from behind Rasher. She's speaking to a man in a state patrol uniform. "Her full name is Ivory Gammon."

Ivory also happens to be the color of her skin, which sets off her strawberry-blond hair. If Halo Man took her, perhaps it was also for other reasons, not just because she saw him kill. She may now be part of his collection of redheaded victims.

I try to stand, but Rasher gently pushes me back down. "You need to talk to the police."

His suspicious gaze is justified. No one here has any idea where I've come from or how I knew about the killing ground.

They need answers, but so do I. "I will, but can I ask you a question?"

Rasher shrugs.

I take it as a yes. "Do you have any Millstone ancestors in your family line?"

He blinks as if that's the strangest thing to ask right now, and it probably is. "No. My mother's maiden name is Osborne."

"What about Lockporte ancestors?"

"Not that I'm aware of."

Maybe my theory about the convergence of Millstone and Lockporte DNA is stupid. I tap my foot as I playback the events of the letter in my head. But I'd only read one. Maybe Ava Millstone can give me more clues. "I need to go to the bathroom."

"Right now?"

"Yes. It's been a long morning. Don't worry, I'll come talk to the police when I'm done."

The state trooper has moved on to questioning the other nurses on the floor. Apparently, he wants to get his facts straight before confronting me.

This time, Rasher doesn't stop me as I get up. I place a hand on his shoulder to let him know he can trust me. I'm not running from this. Then, I head for the bathroom down the hall, knowing he will probably wait outside for me. After secreting myself inside a stall, I pull up the picture of the second letter on my phone. It's dated eight months after the first one. I take a deep breath and begin to read.

CHAPTER 9

December 17, 1872

Dearest Mother,

I must begin this missive by begging you for a response. Since I have not yet received an answering letter, I am in extreme fear for your safety, especially given recent events. As the eve of Christmas approaches, I have much to confess and repent to my Savior. I can only pray that my actions do not bring you pain.

In full view of God, I ended another person's life. A heart which God had set to beating has now ceased through my efforts. And the worst of it shall be that I cannot say I harbor any sorrow for the deed.

On the day I reference, my husband Monroe was plying his furs on a distant trail. As is so often the case, we were alone at our homestead. I was lifting wash to the line whilst eight-year-old Elizabeth wandered around the edge of the woods. She is your granddaughter, Mother, and I will bring her to see you as soon as I am able.

I worked to secure the metal stick pins to the laundry on the drying line. These are more durable than wood and hold more securely in high winds than pegs. They are a luxury, bestowed as a gift to Monroe's former wife by her wealthy parents.

I had completed half of the clothes in the basket when Elizabeth raced back to my side, anxiously telling of finding a black boot in the forest. She has my tendency to imaginative tales, so I smiled at her and searched to find what had incited this idea.

The sight of a man striding out of the woods stole my breath. I knew him at once—my father. He wore a tan overcoat and black boots, the tread of which had inopportunely brought him to Idaho.

"Why have you been keeping yourself from me?" he asked in a tone full of anger.

I leaned down and whispered in Elizabeth's ear. "Go inside, dear love. I will come for you after this person"—I could not call him a gentleman—"leaves our property. Stay there until I come retrieve you."

If only she would have fully listened to me. Or maybe it was a blessing she did not entirely obey. God alone will be the judge of these events.

For the moment, she darted inside. Once she fastened the door behind her, I turned to face the man who had pursued me across no fewer than five states and two territories. His skin displayed the ravages of being exposed to the sun for many days and weeks. Though still strong, his body appeared slimmer.

"Why do you pursue me as a dog hunts after a fox? I am a married woman. A mother with a child. You have no business here."

He was not cowed by my declaration. If anything, he stepped toward me with more boldness. "Married? Truly? Where is the gentleman, in this case."

I did not give him a response. Our portion of the Idaho Territory, nestled up next to the Montana Territory, had its share of strife, but nothing so dangerous as to cause concern. And yet, we are not a careless sort, especially given my experiences on my journey west.

Thus, my hunting rifle leaned against the base of the steps to the house. But it was, sadly, out of reach. I retreated a step, not removing my gaze from this man with some tenuous claim to the title of my father.

Edwin advanced two quick steps.

I thought perhaps I would be better instigating a bluff than a race to my weapon. "I'm going into the house to comfort my daughter. There is no reason for this confrontation, and thus, you should leave. It would be the better situation for both of us."

His gaze flicked to the rifle, then back to me. "You believe I come all this way to merely leave without accomplishing my goal?"

"What goal is that?"

"You belong to me." He put his hands placatingly out as if to calm me with those words. His steps continued to shrink the distance between us.

I had little time to improve my standing in this most difficult contest. "I belong to the good Lord alone. He created me, and I am convinced you had the smallest possible part to play."

With such strong words, I spun around and darted toward the weapon. His heavy steps sounded quick behind me.

My hand brushed the metal of the barrel, but I could not grasp it before he latched on to my bustle from the rear and swung me in a different direction.

I landed on the ground in a heap several paces away. When I glanced up, he stood blocking my way to the rifle. And yet, he did not pick it up. Perhaps he aimed solely to control me, not harm me. I could not help but wonder if he would spirit me away from my daughter or what his plans would be for Elizabeth.

He stepped toward me, and I crawled away backward. If I could not defend myself, I would lead him far from her.

As he grew closer me, I jumped up to sprint.

He lunged.

I swiveled to the side to avoid his grasping hands.

As I spun around, I ran directly into the hanging laundry.

One of Monroe's shirts ripped free from the pins and draped across my face, leaving me blind. A stray pin scratched my cheek.

Edwin leaped onto my back and drove us both into the ground. His weight stole the breath from my lungs. I could not even cry out.

Though I did hear a furtive cry from behind us. "Leave my mother alone."

His weight released me, and I swiped Monroe's shirt off my face. The sight that greeted me stole my breath again. Elizabeth had the rifle in her hands, taking aim at us from the top step of the back porch.

Monroe had just begun to teach her how to handle a weapon, thus I held no confidence in her aim. More to the point, the recoil of the weapon might push her over the opposite side of the steps, injuring her.

Edwin hunched over, looking as if he would run at her at any second.

"Sweet girl, everything will be well. Please put Momma's rifle down."

Confusion knitted her brow. She had always been an obedient child, often wise beyond her years. I could see the warring inside, knowing this man meant no good but wanting to obey her momma. Her hands shook on the weapon, though she did not lower it.

I twisted the laundered shirt in my hands, fumbling for the pin that had scratched my cheek. There was only one way out of this predicament—to stop Edwin myself.

"Do you trust your momma?" I asked Elizabeth.

She nodded immediately.

My fingertips found the pin and yanked it free from the cloth.

"Then, close your eyes, imagine twenty squirrels"—her favorite animal—"and count them slowly. When you open your eyes, all will be well. Trust me."

She gulped once, then obeyed.

Taking advantage of the fact my father kept his focus on Elizabeth, I quietly stood behind him. He took a half step toward her.

I coughed to cause him to turn around. Then, I lunged forward and plunged the long pin into the middle of his throat.

Blood spurted onto my hand, warm and brighter than I expected. Yet, my thoughts were for Elizabeth, not him. I quickly laid him face down on the grass and covered him with Monroe's shirt. In the end, he did make me a murderess, but I kept my daughter innocent.

His death brought me more comfort than I have a right to. The fear of my father had been a winged beast, as if an invisible dragon had long ago sunk its talons into my shoulders. But now, that fear has taken flight to lands far from here. I can live in peace with my daughter and my husband. The Millstone line will continue on within Monroe's family line, the Gammon family.

Consider this missive my confession of deeds to you and God. Thus, I must ask forgiveness for stealing the life of a man you knew, if not loved. I have interfered with his intentions for us, though I still have no knowledge of how he discovered my whereabouts. I fear for you more every day that I do not hear word of your safety. Please write to reassure me on that account.

In all sincerest love,
Ava Fowler Millstone

Librarian's note: Research confirms the death of Alma Walker Millstone at the hands of Edwin Moore in the rural area surrounding Shepherd's Town, West Virginia, on the evening of March 1, 1872, six weeks before Ava Millstone sent her first letter. Both letters were eventually returned to Ava Millstone's family via post by Robert Newman of Shepherd's Town, West Virginia.

CHAPTER 10

THE BATHROOM DOOR SQUEAKS OPEN, bringing me back to the present. Or I mean, the past that is more present than the past I was reading about? Dang, my life is complicated.

Someone wearing dress shoes enters the stall next to me. *Whew.* I'd expected Rasher's heavy boots.

My gaze drops back to the letter displayed on my phone. At least one mystery has been cleared up.

Monroe Gammon. That's the connection. Nurse Ivory Gammon must be a Millstone. So, if I'm actually at the convergence of Millstone and Lockporte again, then who is the Lockporte? Besides myself, of course.

Not Rasher. And hopefully, not the Halo Man. Having a dad who's a con man is preferable to having a serial killer for an ancestor. Though, another rotten apple on the Lockporte ancestral tree wouldn't surprise me.

Speaking of my father, I haven't gotten a handle on the time difference in this leap; it has to be about six hours. Time is passing at home, and I'm probably missing his parole hearing right now. If he gets out to take advantage of more people, it will be partially my fault.

The impact of Ava's story slowly sinks into the cracks in my … my mind? My soul? Wherever. Her father was a terrible man, but when she killed him, she seemed to feel such guilt. Had her father felt any guilt for what he'd done? Probably not. Is guilt only for those who care enough to feel it?

My father has never expressed the emotion, and I doubt any guilt is hiding deep down inside him. Perhaps fighting to keep my father in prison is my way of killing his influence, not just for those people he might con, but for me. To kill his influence in my life.

What would Torri say about it? She'd have a Godly perspective, but who knows what it would be. All I know of God comes from the comparative religions class I took last year.

I wrangle my thoughts back to the facts: Ivory Gammon is a Millstone and possibly connected to Liam. She is missing. And she fits the victimology of half the serial killer's victims.

Those facts roll around in my brain for a few seconds before giving birth to more questions. Why is Halo Man targeting two different types of victims? It's almost like he's two people in one. Dissociative identity disorder comes to mind. Does he really have split personalities, or is he matching one young girl with the woman he imagines her to be when she would grow up? Perhaps he feels the need to symbolically eliminate the whole lifetime of the woman? He must hate women. Or feel intimidated by them.

Without forensic psychology training, I'll never be able to understand what makes a guy like this tick. Plus, I'm getting nowhere hiding in the bathroom. It's time to go face the music.

Rasher and the state trooper are waiting when I open the bathroom door. The officer is a man with a small paunch—probably from riding around in his patrol car too much—and a receding hairline—definitely from his mother's genetics. His name tag reads Trooper Vargas.

I could blame my long bathroom break on the stress of the

situation, but that might make me look guilty. "Sorry. Must have been something I ate."

The trooper rolls his eyes. "State your name."

"Mars Lockporte."

He writes it down while saying, "Lockporte. Sounds vaguely familiar."

"That's what I thought when I heard it too," Rasher says. "But I can't place the name."

"I may have some family on my dad's side from Idaho."

The trooper asks what happened, so I relate the basics of my time in the hospital and the library. He writes it all down in his notebook.

Finally, I bend my neck to get the trooper's attention as he's still writing in his notebook. "I'm worried about Nurse Gammon. I want to go check her house to see if she went back there."

Trooper Vargas trains his gaze on me. "You know Ivory Gammon?"

"No, not really. She offered to let Daisy stay at her house."

The trooper raises his eyebrows.

"A dog," Rasher clarifies.

"Anyway," I say with a tinge of annoyance, "maybe she went back there to check on the dogs."

The trooper defers to Rasher, who says, "You've got interviews to finish here. I'll go with him."

As I descend the hospital front steps for the second time that day, I grab Rasher's arm. "Thanks for standing up for me in there."

He stops and stares at my hand for a few seconds, then shakes his head. "I did no such thing. You always seem to be at the center of trouble. That either makes you extremely unlucky or a killer in your own right. I'm making sure you don't run off until we figure out which one you are."

"Fair enough. Trust me, I'm the unlucky one."

He side-eyes me. "Good. Because I'd hate to be forced to shoot a hole in my favorite shirt."

Rasher lets me lead on the walk to Ivory's house since he's apparently never been there. As our steps pound in unison, I'm struck by how little I know about this guy.

Might as well start with a big question. "Rasher, do you believe in God?"

"Of course. I go to church every Sunday."

"What does God do for you?"

He gives a slight laugh. "He created me, for one thing." His tone then becomes serious. "And I believe he helps me through stuff."

Is he talking about physical stuff like his diabetes? Or something deeper? "Like an emotional support animal?"

This earns me a quizzical look. "More like a wise father. Mine died last year."

"He was a good man?"

"The best."

Maybe that's why I have such issues with God, issues that other people don't seem to have. I'm suspicious of most older men. Say *wise father* to me and I want to know what his angle is. But Rasher isn't like that. Nor was Long. Granted, neither of them has been much older than me.

When we get close to Ivory's house, I remember one of the few clues I have on the killer that I haven't followed up on. "Rasher, do you know anyone who wrestles and has a deformed ear from it?"

He chuckles. "Anyone in town who wrestled would have those cauliflower ears."

"Someone with medium brown hair?"

"Well, I guess there's a few who fit the description. Charlie Reed, Allen Lund, and maybe Archie Gordon. Why do you ask?"

I dip my head sheepishly. "I may have caught a glimpse of someone else when I was out there in the woods originally. Someone other than Gerald Morgan."

He puts his fists on his hips. "What? Why didn't you tell me before?"

"I wasn't sure who to trust." I raise one brow at him to emphasize my next point. "I'm following my gut and trusting you now."

He still looks angry, and his silence for the rest of the way confirms it. But at least I have three other suspects now. After we find Ivory, I can search for these guys and see who might have a halo.

As we approach the house, I almost stumble on the first block of concrete leading to her doorway because alarm bells are ringing in my head. The front door stands open about six inches. She'd firmly closed it to lock the dogs in when we left. If she came back to check on them, she wouldn't leave it open.

A deep bark sounds. Baxter darts around from the backyard. I put a hand out to him, and he calms down. He gives me a quick sniff, then lets me kneel to pet him.

"What's going on, boy?" I call out toward the backyard, "Daisy?"

No response. Baxter fidgets on his feet.

I stop petting him to yell for Daisy again, but clearly she's run off. Annoyed with me, Baxter paws at my arm to get me to soothe him once more. His nails catch on the towel wrapped around my CRASH device, ripping the fabric off. He stomps to try to dislodge it from his paw, grinding it into the muddy dirt at the edge of the flower bed. Great. I won't be putting that back on.

"Nurse Gammon?" Rasher calls into the house as he enters.

I follow behind him with Baxter following behind me. Though I was in here a couple of hours ago, this feels like I'm intruding.

The inside of her house is as organized and tidy as I remember with one exception. A basket on the floor has been overturned, spilling shoes onto the hardwoods. Next to the basket lies an apricot-colored scrunchie—just like the ones at the crime scene. My chest tightens. Never did I imagine that a hair tie would fill me with such dread.

Rasher picks it up. "Before today, I've never seen such an accessory. It can't be a coincidence."

"The killer took her," I reply. Rasher spent more time at the crime scene than I did. "What does he do with these?"

He sucks in a deep breath before answering. "I think he strangles the young girls with them. But all the bodies had them."

"Maybe he carries them with him all the time, as part of a killing kit. Looks like they came back here for shoes."

Rasher stares out Ivory's back window. "He's probably taking her to the mountains."

I move toward the door. "We have to let the police know."

But Rasher hesitates. "We don't have proof that anything has happened to her. She might have come back on her own, accidentally let Daisy go, and possibly changed shoes to go look for the dog."

A plausible theory, but my instincts say he's wrong. Fortunately, his bias against women being killers keeps him from coming up with the alternative I presented to Nurse Hughes—that Ivory killed Serenity Brooks and is now on the run. The Ivory Gammon I met wouldn't hurt anyone. Then again, I've been fooled before, by my own father, in fact.

I rub Baxter's head a beat while waiting for Rasher to make a decision. When he still doesn't move after a few seconds, I insist, "If she did go after a dog, she would have called the hospital first to let them know so others could cover her patients."

He places the scrunchie back where he found it and joins me at the door. "You're right. We need to ask the nurses."

We could call from here, but it will be easier to make sure we don't miss talking to any of the nurses if we go back to the hospital. The alternative would mean passing the phone around in the style of the game Telephone and hoping to reach them all.

After locking Baxter in the house, we head back to the

hospital at a faster pace. With every quick stride, my fear for Ivory grows. If Halo Man took her, I'm several steps behind the curve. I don't know who he is. And I have no clue where to start looking for her.

CHAPTER 11

As we near the hospital, I glance over at the man with me. He's not Halo Man, but could he be working with Halo Man? My instincts say he isn't a part of this, but my brain is still going in circles. Rasher didn't confess his diabetes to the trooper. Maybe he didn't realize Serenity's death is a possible insulin overdose? Or maybe he's keeping the info to himself to avoid looking guilty.

He says he came back to the hospital for supplies, but what if he never left? He could have stayed in a janitor's closet somewhere, waiting until Serenity's room was free of visitors and staff. But then, he would have no reason to admit his diabetes to me after killing her.

No matter which way I turn things, Rasher doesn't fit as a killer.

In the hospital, we find Nurse Hughes in a room with the door open, taking a catheter out of a patient. So much for privacy in 1972.

Nurse Hughes claims that as the senior member of the nursing staff on site, Ivory would have contacted her if she had to leave unexpectedly. Since Ivory hasn't been heard from, Nurse Hughes makes it clear she's very concerned. We check with each and every other nurse to be sure Ivory didn't contact one of them and they forgot to relay the message. In the end, Rasher and I are convinced Ivory's disappearance is not of her own accord.

By the time we finish talking to the nurses, Serenity has been dead for two hours. We travel down the hall, and my empty stomach lurches at the sight of her through the still open doorway. She's lying there alone with a sheet over her body.

Nurse Hughes tells us the hospital has finished preliminary tests on the contents of the syringe. Rasher approaches Trooper Vargas and hooks a thumb toward the room. "Did you find out what killed Ms. Brooks?"

"Most likely an excess of insulin," the trooper says, "since that's the substance left in the syringe. We're waiting for the coroner to take her to the morgue. An autopsy will tell us what truly killed her."

While saying this, Trooper Vargas stares at me as if trying to gauge my reaction, but I'm staring at Rasher. Too much of a coincidence for Serenity to die from a chemical he injects into his body. And yet, Rasher's expression holds no guilt, only suspicion … of me.

I'm the first one in this suspicion circle to break the silence. "I couldn't have harmed her. I was—"

"At the library," Trooper Vargas says. "I heard you the first time." His tone isn't confirming my innocence. Anything but. "Where are you from, Mr. Lockporte?"

"Colorado." At least the state of Colorado exists in this time, unlike during my last leap to the Civil War.

"And where are you staying while in town?"

"Uh …"

The trooper scoffs. "Just another hippie traveling the country with no roots. We have a term for people like you—homeless vagrants."

"I'm no vagrant." I can't argue with the homeless adjective, at least not in this time period.

Should I bring Rasher's medicine to the trooper's attention?

Maybe Rasher wants his diabetes kept private. I don't think he's a killer, but what if I'm wrong?

"Why are you in town, Mr. Lockporte?"

Trooper Vargas's question should have a simple answer, and yet nothing appropriate comes to mind. *I might be in town to stop a serial killer, except I'm doing a poor job of it? Or I might be in town to figure out how to bring my friend back?* None of the truthful answers will keep me from being detained, and will possibly get me arrested or committed.

I rack my brain for a more acceptable answer, but then I catch sight of something behind the trooper, and my thoughts are suddenly scattered like confetti whipped around by a tornado.

It can't be.

The squiggly gray matter in my head has gone soft because of what I see—a familiar white glow.

I lean around the officer, but a nurse walks by and blocks my view of the area.

The trooper mimics my movements to lean in my direction, trying to capture my attention.

"Sorry," I say. "Thought I saw someone I knew."

"A person from Colorado?"

"I don't know." I shake my head. "My mistake." *Focus, Mars.* "Uh, you're right, Officer. I'm just traveling around, exploring our great country."

The trooper shakes his head. "Waste of time. Why don't you try contributing …"

I tune out his lecture, not because it's rude and judgmental, even though it is, but because the glow emanates from over the trooper's shoulder again. I glimpse a man walking along the hall toward us. Correction, *the* man is walking toward us. His halo defines his outline, even in the bright fluorescent lighting.

My breath hitches. Ivory may still be missing, but the killer is here.

CHAPTER 12

University of Colorado Boulder
September 20, 2051
10:30 p.m.

TORRI STEALTHILY ENTERS the hallway from the stairwell. No sense alerting anyone besides Ellis to her presence since she doesn't have a valid reason to be here. The door to Mars's office is open, and light spills into the hallway. She quickens her pace. Is he back? She spent the whole day—when she wasn't at work—at his house waiting for him to return. Earlier this evening, it clicked that this probably wasn't the first time he'd traveled. He disappeared for almost a whole day the day before. At that time, his friend, Kiefer, had given her the code to let her in to take care of Mars's animals.

If the last disappearance can be used as a guideline, it may still be a while before he returns, but waiting isn't her strong suit. Besides, Mars told her how a lot of the physics department likes to keep late hours.

At the doorway, Torri freezes with one hand on the doorjamb. Disappointment crowds her gut. It's not Mars. Akane sits in his chair with her back to the door and her fingers clicking away on his keyboard. This isn't right.

Akane hasn't heard her approach, so Torri focuses on the screen. Lines of code spill down it like a waterfall of foreign symbols. She can't interpret them, much less read them at the speed they are streaming by.

Akane's words from earlier come back to her. *Best that you don't tell anyone. No one would believe it anyway.*

But Akane had no trouble believing her eyes when Mars disappeared, had seemed to expect it, in fact. She knows more about what's going on.

Torri clears her throat. "Sabotage much?"

Akane jumps and gasps, then returns her fingers to the keyboard without even looking around. "Don't scare me like that. How did you get in here so late?"

The woman is deflecting a question with a question. Torri's instincts scream at her to dig into this, but she has no more right to be here than Akane.

Finally, she replies, "Ellis let me in."

This gets a slight turn of the head and one raised eyebrow. "Of course he did."

Torri suppresses a laugh. Maybe if Akane tried being nicer, people would do more things for her. But she seems like the sort of person who prefers to pit herself against the world.

Taking a tip from her interview tactics class, Torri drops her backpack on the floor and sits down on the only other available seat—the base of the trellis—while keeping silent. People are more likely to open up when the silence stretches and grows, pushing against the elephant in the room. And even though Akane probably knows Torri can't read the code, if she's doing something illegal or unethical, subconsciously she won't want to keep doing it in the presence of someone else.

Akane's fingers go still. "What are you doing?"

Torri folds her arms and smiles, though Akane hasn't even turned around. "Waiting for you to tell me what you're doing."

At last, she turns in the chair, quietly assessing with her lovely, dark, suspicious eyes. "How long have you known Mars?"

The one chink in Torri's armor, and Akane found it with the speed of an experienced interrogator. Mars and Torri met not even forty-eight hours ago when she came to his house to check on a "pet" armadillo, though it seems much longer. But again, this is a manipulation tactic. A distraction.

With a flourish, Akane sweeps her arms around to place her elbows on her knees. She leans toward Torri, a sympathetic expression on her tanned face. "You don't know what it's like to date a serious scientist, do you?"

"Uh, no."

The few men she'd dated were in business or criminal justice. Intelligent men, but not genius level. And all were short relationships. Well, except for Mason, but she hadn't been able to trust anything he said.

"Scientists care only about the work. Using their brains gives them a superiority high. They will always dump you for the next intellectual pursuit. And they will always think they're smarter than you. Why put up with that?"

Funny, now that she mentions it, rather than being intimidating, Mars's brain is the sexiest thing about him. And that is saying a lot since Torri got a good look at his six pack a couple of times. Man, the guy is toned. She bites her cheek to keep in her smile. "We're not dating."

"Oh, sweetie. Don't fool yourself. You're already hooked. But you need to run while you still can."

Torri narrows her eyes at the deeper meaning in Akane's words. Not only does she want Torri to go away, but she harbors something underneath. She's projecting her own insecurities onto Mars. Her desire to achieve is more than validation. It's a protective wall. "Were you bullied as a child for your sunny disposition?"

Akane sits back and blinks, as if Torri smacked her. Definitely hit a nerve. After a second of open-mouthed gaping, Akane schools her features and shrugs. "Don't say I didn't warn you."

Then, she lifts gracefully out of the chair and strides from the room. Probably on her way to get security.

At least she gave up on Mars's computer for now. But he'd better come back soon, before Akane manipulates his entire doctoral thesis. Or worse, what if she ruins his chance at coming back?

Ravalli County Hospital
August 30, 1972
6:00 p.m.

TROOPER VARGAS CONTINUES TALKING without noticing my unusual reaction. But Rasher isn't so clueless. He turns to see what has shredded me. He gives a small nod to the man who is passing by. Brown hair. Medium build. Gold watch peeking out from beneath the sleeve of a light brown Henley.

The man smiles at Rasher, then the officer. When he catches my eye, he stumbles, but quickly rights himself.

He recognizes me. Does he realize that I recognize him?

As he turns his head away, his chin-length hair brushes back from his face, briefly exposing the deformed ear. It's definitely the same man from the clearing.

Without making eye contact again, he continues to walk toward the stairwell.

"Who is that?" I ask.

"Allen Lund," the trooper says. "He works here in the lab."

Allen Lund. One of the names Rasher gave me. "He's not wearing scrubs or a lab coat. Why is he here?"

The trooper stabs his pencil into his notebook. "How should I know? Maybe he's picking up his paycheck or something."

True, this is a time period when people don't have instant

access to funds. I suppress the urge to run a hand through my hair. Lifting my arm might cause the officer to notice my CRASH device. I haven't looked at it in a while, and now wouldn't be the time to check the Risk Assessment function for what I'm about to do.

"Excuse me. I need some air."

The trooper narrows his gaze. "Aren't you the one who led the rangers to the burial ground?"

"Those victims weren't given the courtesy of burial, but yes, I saw them in the woods and then led the rangers back to them." I cover my heart with a hand. "It was quite a shock. I've never seen anything like that."

"How about you hang around and help us find out what happened to them, then? After all, none of the victims seem to be local. You should want to help your fellow *free spirits*."

"I just need some fresh air. I'll come back to talk to you."

"What were you doing in the woods?" Rasher asks.

I take a small step backward, in the direction where Allen Lund has gone. The men step along with me.

"I was looking for wildlife."

Both men raise their brows. Rasher purses his lips, probably because I originally told him I had a fight with a girlfriend. Nothing like a shifting story to draw doubt my way.

Best to feed into the stereotype. "You know, moose, elk, and deer. That's what us hippies do, Officer."

He lowers his brows, and his forehead smooths. I take another step backward. This time, neither man follows. The trooper knows he doesn't have enough to hold me. I'm just a guy in the wrong place at the right time, breaking open a serial killer case.

When I turn to follow Allen, he's nowhere to be seen. He could have ducked into another room, but he'd likely try to escape from the building. The fastest way would be down the stairwell. I push open the door to the stairs and listen. Sure enough, footsteps sound on the landing below.

On my tiptoes, I quietly descend.

Working as a lab tech is a noble profession in my time. But perhaps it wasn't always that way. Maybe working in the hospital as something other than a doctor causes Allen to feel less accepted by women. It would be hard to deal with being around women all day who think of him as inferior to the doctors who roam the halls.

As a hospital employee, Allen would have had access to Serenity's room, and he would have known what to do to give her an overdose of insulin. But if he did that to her hours ago, he would have worn his hospital garb to avoid suspicion and left immediately afterward. So why would he come back in plain clothes? To gauge the police response?

All of this begs the other looming question: Where is Ivory Gammon? Did he kill her and stuff her body somewhere before coming back? Or does he have her stashed away? Maybe at his house?

The trooper's recent words resonate in my head. *None of the victims seem to be local.* That probably means the killer is local. No sense hunting in your own backyard. But that would also mean that if Allen took Ivory, she would be the first victim known to him. He'd be taking quite a risk.

I make it to the bottom of the creaky stairs without seeing anyone. He could have gone out the side door or through the interior door leading back into the hospital. After seeing me, I'm guessing he wants to get away.

Turns out, I'm partially correct. He went out the side door, but he didn't leave immediately. As soon as I open the door, a brick comes flying at my head. I duck in time to miss the full force of it, but it scrapes the top of my scalp.

He backs away as I charge out the door.

"Who are you?" he yells.

"Where is Ivory?" I yell back.

He's running away from me in reverse. "I don't know. You've got the wrong guy."

I stop and so does he. We stare at each other warily from several feet apart.

"You were with the bodies," I say.

He shakes his head. "Only because I got a call from a friend who told me to come out there."

Allen's halo flickers for a second before returning to full force. Is it just a trick of the light? Or does that mean he's lying? "Who is this friend?"

"I can't tell you that."

Wanting to protect a friend is one thing, protecting a murderer is a whole different beast. "Why didn't you report the killing ground to the police, then?"

"And say what? That I had nothing to do with it, but there's a whole bunch of bodies in the woods? I would be the first person they accused."

He's not wrong because that is exactly what happened to me, which is why I can't let this guy go, despite the halo. I take another step to close the distance between us.

Too late, I register the second brick that he'd concealed behind his back. I dodge to the left to avoid his swing.

He swipes the arc wider, catching me on the temple. I crumple like a sack of garbage, but I stay conscious. Allen leans over me, brick still in his grip. The murderous look on his face reveals his intent to bash my skull in.

The door clangs as someone tries to open it. It's blocked by the first thrown brick, which fell vertical on the ground outside. Allen flinches and scowls at the door.

He throws the brick at my head while he runs away.

I easily shift to avoid the hit just as Rasher shoves the door open. "Mars, what happened to you?"

I don't answer. I just stare at the corner of a far building, around which Allen disappeared. Ivory's life is at risk if I can't find him again. Why does this evil guy have the halo anyway? Hopefully, it doesn't mean that I have to somehow save him to accomplish my goal of saving Liam.

CHAPTER 13

Trooper Vargas has his arms crossed over his paunch. His disbelieving glare is directed at me like it could pierce my heart. "How do you know this man you saw is the killer?"

I squirm in a tiny chair in the tiny conference room off the patient wing. "When I was out in the woods the first night, I saw someone else out there."

"No one has mentioned that," the trooper complains. It seems directed at Rasher, but he doesn't take the bait.

"I-I didn't see his face," I reply.

"Then how do you know that guy is Allen Lund?" he asks.

"Because Allen Lund just attacked me."

"That doesn't mean squat. He could have attacked you because you chased him."

"I didn't chase him. I *followed* him. And Allen was waiting for me. He must have recognized me too."

The trooper rolled his eyes. "Why did you follow him?"

"I caught a glimpse of his wrestler's ear. And the way he moved was familiar."

Rasher finally speaks up. "Do the other people who work here have any opinions of him?"

Vargas seems to consider this. Probably because the question came from Rasher and not me.

"Let me ask a few nurses," the trooper says. "Keep an eye on him."

Rasher and I wait in uncomfortable silence while he questions several nurses. Hopefully, Nurse Hughes doesn't tell him I thought Ivory might be the killer.

When Vargas returns, his mouth is twisted into a frown. "The nurses call him All Hands Allen for the way he comes on to them, finding excuses to touch them in inappropriate places, but that's no reason to suspect him of murder. They also say he keeps to himself and never causes trouble."

Practically a serial killer's dossier. I slap my palms on my jeans. "What if he did something to Serenity and Nurse Gammon caught him, so he took her?"

Several heartbeats pass with set jaws and hard eyes staring at me from both men.

Finally, Vargas sighs. "I need to stay here to handle this death investigation." He shifts toward Rasher. "Do you want to entertain this wild pony and go to Mr. Lund's residence to ensure everything is as it should be?"

Wild pony? Does he mean me or my theory? It doesn't matter as long as one of them goes to check.

Rasher nods a little too quickly, stands, and grabs his backpack. Perhaps he senses I'm telling the truth. Or maybe he knows something about Allen Lund that I don't.

After getting Allen's address from the main hospital office, we head down the front stairs to Rasher's truck, parked at the curb. As I open the door to get in, another frightening thought works its way down my spine, clinging to me like a wet blanket.

I had my suspicions of Rasher before deciding he isn't working with Lund, but what if someone else is? Someone who is more partner than accomplice.

Two rows of victims.

Two manners of killing—strangulation and slitting the throat.

Two different ages of victims—young adult and prepubescent.

In this time period, knowledge of crime scene analysis, DNA, and victimology is limited. My knowledge is limited too. I only know what my sister Gaia rattled off to me from her crime-junkie shows, but that's enough to realize the sum total of the evidence points to the rarest possibility—two different killers working together.

Since I have no clue why the halo has shown up on only one person so far, I can't speculate whether a halo would also be found on Allen's partner. If that person doesn't have a halo, I wouldn't recognize them. It could be anyone. This is all assuming Allen doesn't have some sort of split personality, which I haven't ruled out.

Rasher throws a frown my way. Oh, I haven't closed my door yet. I yank it closed, and we take off.

My internal wrestling match with the facts must show on my face because he asks, "What really makes you think Allen Lund is the killer? And don't tell me it's just the way he moves. You asked about ears earlier, but that's not all you've got, right?"

I can't tell him about the halo, but I have one more piece of evidence. "I recognized his watch. It's gold and flashy."

Come to think of it, the watch looks similar to one my grandfather had passed down to me—the one I lost on a riverbank in 1862. Surely, Allen Lund isn't a Lockporte. I didn't get a good enough look that night or at the hospital to determine if it's the same watch. Plus, my dad's family has ties to Idaho, not Montana, at least not that I'm aware of.

The drive to Allen's house takes less than ten minutes, but it seems like an hour with how keyed up I am. Eventually, we arrive at a quaint ranch house with sage-green shutters. Oddly homey for a serial killer. But if Allen had been in the woods innocently, in the wrong place at the wrong time like me, then he wouldn't have shot at me in the woods or turned murderous just because I followed him out of the hospital. Unless he *is* innocent and thinks I'm the killer. This isn't helping. I'm going in circles.

We get out and approach the door. Rasher rings the doorbell several times with no answer.

When he begins knocking, I say, "I'll go look around back."

I circle the property, checking doors and windows and looking for hints of life. Nothing. The place is buttoned up tight. No way in. Legally, that is.

I start to head back around front, but then I catch sight of something on the ground. If it hadn't been such a light color, I would have missed it peeking between the blades of grass. Smashed down and abandoned is a light pink scrunchie.

I pick it up and come around to the front to find Rasher examining something else on the ground at the side of the house, near the driveway.

"She's not in there," he says. "Not anymore."

He's kneeling and pointing at two deep furrows in the long grass. Drag marks that end right next to wheel marks. Except there's three wheel marks, not four. Maybe from an ATV?

"So, she walked inside," he says, "then he did something to her and dragged her out."

When I show Rasher the scrunchie, he merely nods as if confirming this is our guy. At least we are on the same page now.

"Maybe he drugged her here and stashed her so that he could go back to the hospital," I say. "But why would he need to go back?"

Rasher stands to his full height. "Not for his paycheck. Trooper Vargas checked. Payday isn't until next week. Maybe he wanted to grab the needle before it was discovered?"

Except the needle with the diabetes medication points toward Rasher, not Allen. Why would Allen need to come back for it unless he was protecting Rasher? *Ugh.* I'm back to suspecting him again.

I peer into Rasher's face, looking deep into his eyes. Is he fooling me? He doesn't have a CRASH implant, so I can't ask to see his HF—Honesty function—but most of us have a deep seated intuition when it comes to whether people are lying to us. We just tend to have trouble interpreting that instinct, which means I can use the Risk Assessment function of my CRASH implant to help me decide if I can trust Rasher.

I'll have to be direct. "Are you working with Allen to kill people?"

Rasher blinks at me several times. He might be genuinely surprised. Or he might be stalling for what to say.

After scrutinizing me for a moment, he replies, "No. I've been trying to figure out if you are. Or if Allen is even involved at all."

With a swipe of my hand through my hair, I glance at my CRASH device. It's a welcome shade of lavender—light red for low risk and light blue for high perceived reward. The artificial intelligence in my device has interpreted my subconscious biochemical signals in a way that suggests, deep down, I trust what Rasher just said.

"What is that thing?" he asks.

"I told you. A tattoo." At least, it's flat enough to look like one. "Kind of like a mood ring."

Rasher shakes his head. "What kind of ring?"

I shrug. Maybe they haven't been invented yet. "Never mind." I've confirmed Rasher is probably innocent. Time to get back on track. "Did you notice there wasn't enough blood at the site we found? He doesn't kill his victims there. So where would Allen take Nurse Gammon if he intended to kill her?"

His intense dark eyes shift to the side as he makes the connections I'm implying. Not enough blood at the dumping ground, plus no signs of struggle. Even without the advantages of modern criminal justice theory, this man is a born investigator. "Somewhere sheltered where he would have full control."

"Not outside?"

"No. A scream can echo among the mountains for quite a

ways. He would want to keep things contained. So only he could hear her cries."

I turn and look at the house. "We have to get in there to find a hint of where he might go."

Rasher is tapping his foot as he thinks. "Maybe not."

"What do you mean?"

"Park rangers are tasked with checking on the half dozen unused park buildings from time to time. Usually, it's Brenda's responsibility, but a few months ago, she was sick for several days, and I was bored. I decided to check on them all. The one that's farthest away, Wiles Station near Wiles Peak, showed evidence of someone having been there. You can only get to it on foot, on horseback"—he gestures at the vehicle marks on the ground—"or by ATV."

"What kind of evidence?"

"A dirty towel left in the wash basin. And ATV tire tracks outside. Nothing was damaged, so I just told Brenda. She said she would keep an eye out for anything unusual there on her rounds."

"That has to be it. Can we walk there?"

Rasher shakes his head. "Not quickly. It's miles away, uphill, through the forest." He jerks a thumb over his shoulder in the direction of Allen's detached garage. "But we could borrow his other ATV."

Sure enough, the wheel of a vehicle is just visible under the partially opened garage door. "Sounds great. Let's find the keys."

CHAPTER 14

IT TOOK HALF an hour to find the keys to the ATV. The man door to the garage was open, but they weren't in there, which meant they had to be in the house. We searched several minutes for a way in before I remembered Ivory's hidden key. Allen didn't have any garden gnomes, so I started checking random rocks. Rasher was just about to break a window when I found it under a rock by the garage.

Inside the house, the key to Allen's second ATV waited conveniently in a bowl in the kitchen.

With the key in hand, as I'm lifting up the roll-top garage door, something occurs to me. I stop and turn toward Rasher. "Why does he have two?"

"Excuse me?"

"Who needs two ATVs?"

"Sometimes folks around here have a backup or an extra one for when friends come to hunt with them."

"Or when you want to torture and kill together?" I say sarcastically.

"It is suspicious. But if he has a partner, they didn't head out with him from here this time."

I push the door the rest of the way up. "Plus, if we take the ATV, then the partner can't get there to back him up."

With a curt nod, Rasher takes the key and climbs on.

"Do you think you should call this in?" I ask.

"All we have are drag marks. We don't know for sure that he has her. Or even that he will be at the Wiles Station. It will take too long to explain our theory to the troopers." He grabs the walkie-talkie on his shoulder. "But I can bring some backup of our own."

He gets ahold of Ranger Morrow and asks her to take the park ATV and meet us at the Wiles ranger's station. He only tells her it's a possible abduction situation.

After he's done, I climb on the seat behind him. "Is it too dangerous to bring her in on this?"

"You mean she might end up being a target because of her reddish hair? I thought of that too, but she's armed and capable. Besides, it's a little too late to take it back now. Once she's on her way, she wouldn't likely hear her radio over the ATV's engine."

We leave from a trail in the backyard, which starts out with tall pine trees flanking us on both sides. A short time later, we break out onto a ridge. A valley stretches before us, dotted with patches of grass and pine trees. A blue-gray mountain stands majestically in the background. I resist the urge to grab my phone and take a picture of the unspoiled beauty. The CRASH device was difficult enough to explain away.

Rasher sweeps a hand toward the mountain. "Medicine Point. We are going to skirt around the base of it and come up on the north side of Wiles Peak. Brenda will be coming in from the east."

The position of the sun in the sky gives me pause. Will we make it there before dark? A night approach throws the odds in favor of the killer. He could ambush us anywhere along the trail. But we can't afford to wait. Ivory's life could be at stake.

On the ride up and down the terrain, my arms are fully gripping Rasher around his sternum, which is difficult because of the backpack on his back, but my mind wanders, working on the multitude of problems brought by this strange leap. Will saving Ivory Gammon save Liam? Or maybe the halo means I have to save Allen Lund to save Liam? Is there some ripple effect that Allen will have if he stays alive? But that doesn't make sense. He can't father any children if he's in jail. And I won't let him go free, given the danger he poses to women.

Just because the halo meant I was supposed to save Long Browning during the Civil War, that doesn't necessarily mean I'm supposed to save Allen. Statistically speaking, Long's case is a sample size of one, which is insignificant. So why can't I shake the feeling that I need to rescue Allen too?

No matter what, I won't protect Allen at the expense of Ivory.

After about an hour, Rasher twists his neck to yell back at me. "Why did you say you had a fight with your girlfriend when I first asked you?"

Of course he won't let such a discrepancy go. "Having an imaginary fight with a girlfriend sounds better than saying I drift from town to town. I'm a wanderer, not a vagrant."

He turns his head toward the front without comment. Guess he's accepted my explanation.

Another hour later, we pass through a wider valley, lush with trees flanked by a dry creek bed, then we head uphill once again. Rasher cuts the engine halfway up the slope, angling the machine so it doesn't slide downhill.

"I haven't seen any signs of his vehicle in a while. But he may have come here along a different route. If he's at the ranger's station, he will hear the ATV if we get much closer. It's best not to push it. We'll walk the rest of the way."

I've heard no other ATVs to indicate Ranger Morrow is on her way. But if she's coming in from the other direction, maybe I wouldn't hear it.

Normally, the verdant pine forest with a knob of a mountain rising behind it would be lovely and inspiring, maybe even remind me of home in Boulder. Tonight, though, the setting sun brings out every shadow and defines every crevice, creating an eerie, foreign landscape.

Rasher must be wondering about Brenda too, because he taps the walkie-talkie button twice—some sort of signal to her.

She must have been taking a break or going slow enough on the ATV to hear because she answers in a raspy voice. "I'm going off trail now from Warm Springs Creek to Wiles Creek and straight up. ETA thirty minutes."

"Copy that. We will be there sooner. We are going in," Rasher says to her. To me, he whispers, "That will be one heck of a shortcut. But we can't wait for her."

"It might be for the best," I reply, "given that we already have one redheaded woman in danger."

He strips the backpack from his shoulders and digs around for a few seconds before coming out with some sort of pistol. I'm not very familiar with guns, even though I had to fire a musket on my last leap.

He holds the gun by his side, hikes his backpack back on, then turns to me. "If things go unexpected in there and the worst happens to me, please find my mom up near Billings to let her know what happened. She … uh … moves around a lot like you, so I don't know if the forest service will be able to find her."

"Of course." But I shouldn't make this promise. I probably won't be around to notify anyone for him.

"What about you? Anyone I can contact?"

The question hits hard. Anyone who cares about me lives eighty years in the future. I'm all alone here, though my best estimate would indicate that will be the case for only a few more hours. My stomach rumbles, reminding me that food has been available, though not a priority, on this leap.

"No one," I finally reply.

He merely shrugs, not surprised a hippie like me has no family. I haven't even figured out if there's a Lockporte in this leap, but what matters most is my theory that Liam is related to a Millstone—Ivory. Something I did in my first leap must have caused Ivory to be here and be in danger. Likely, it was getting Carlton and Francis killed so Alma Millstone, their mother, begins to search for her only other relative, her daughter, Ava, who then flees to this area to escape her father. This led to Ivory's birth in Montana, where she is kidnapped and killed before she can give birth to Liam's great-grandparent.

When we break from the darkness of the trees about fifteen minutes later, I blink at the quaintness of the little log cabin with a grass sod roof. The windowpanes have muntins in them, for goodness' sake. Surely, this isn't where a sadistic killer brings his victims to strangle or stab them? And yet, my core begins to tingle with awareness, or maybe vibrate is the right word.

It's the halo. It has to be. He's in there, and the cells in my body are reacting to the proximity on a quantum level.

Rasher takes a step toward the cabin while raising his gun about thirty degrees.

I put a hand on his arm. "Be careful. He's in there."

"How do you know?"

Yeah, how do I know? I swallow before pushing out the lie. "I saw movement at the window."

A dog's bark startles both of us. It came from inside the log cabin. I hadn't been looking for evidence of a dog in Allen's house. We simply found the keys and rushed back out.

"Pepper!" a man yells.

Thank goodness he doesn't realize the dog is trying to warn him. Or maybe he's distracted by what he's doing.

"We have to get in there," I say.

Before Rasher can answer, a woman's scream rents the air.

CHAPTER 15

Rasher enters the cabin first with his gun angled slightly down. I follow, peering over his shoulder. The space consists of one room lit by an antique-looking battery-powered lantern.

The scene inside is exactly as horrific as I expect, and yet, my expectations are turned on their head. Allen Lund grips a long-bladed knife in his left fist. Blood coats the handle and drips down onto his wrist and the floor. The droplets stain the raw wood a deep merlot.

More blood forms a brown amoeba-like stain on a tan sofa where Ivory must have been lying. But she's alive!

Still wearing her nursing uniform, now with hiking boots, she's cowering on the other side of the room behind a chair with her hand pressed to her neck. Blood seeps through her fingertips.

Amazingly, the dog wasn't trying to warn Allen about us. A large black setter stands between Allen and Ivory, snarling at *him*. Apparently, he's never taken his dog on a kill mission before, and the dog is having none of it.

"Good boy, Pepper," I mutter.

A blast of realization slams into me. *Pep.* Serenity was trying to tell me the dog's name. Maybe this dog has been along before. Maybe he helped Serenity escape.

A gun rests on the kitchen counter, out of Allen's reach. His weapon is no match for Rasher's pistol.

"Put down the knife," Rasher commands.

Instead, Allen puts his hands up in a gesture of surrender. He flips the knife so his fingers grip the dull side of the blade as he raises it high.

When his gaze meets mine, he sucks in a shallow breath. "Are you a ghost?"

"What?"

"You have some sort of aura around you."

He's serious. He can see a halo around *me*. Long never said anything about seeing it. But then again, Long had seemed unusually willing to trust me, to the point of sacrificing himself for me. I thought it was just in his character, but what if it was more? What if he also felt the quantum draw of a halo surrounding me? Maybe that was how he always seemed to find me when we got separated.

The halo around Allen falters, blinking in and out in undulating waves, similar to what I saw with Long toward the end of my leap. What in the world does that mean now? Just that the time is growing short? I take a step closer, lured by the halo itself. Certainty takes root in my core. I have to protect this man, to keep him alive. If only I understood why.

Allen's arm twitches. The protective feeling morphs into a tingle of alarm. Before Rasher can shoot, Allen whips his arm down, sending the knife flying straight at Rasher's chest.

On instinct, I shove Rasher to the side to minimize the knife wound and to ensure that when he gets hit, he won't shoot Allen.

The gun goes off. Splinters of wood rain down from the ceiling.

Ivory screams and ducks farther behind the chair.

Rasher's gun goes flying as the knife embeds itself in his flesh. My shove caused the knife to hit him in the right arm rather than the chest.

I saved them both, for the moment. But at what cost? Allen is scrambling after Rasher's gun.

Pepper resumes barking, standing guard over Ivory. But another, more distant barking has joined his yaps of distress. Another dog is outside?

Not important.

I dive on the floor, trying to get to the gun first.

His hand closes over the barrel. But he doesn't have time to lift it before I slam into him. I won't let him die, but I also won't let him kill anyone, either.

We tumble for a few seconds, then hit the unforgiving wood wall, hard. The gun slides with us.

Though I'm bigger and stronger than Allen, he's wiry, so he shimmies around my limbs. By the time I strike out at him, he has one hand on the gun.

I elbow him in the face. His head cracks against the center of a wooden log in the wall. The halo around him flickers out. Did I hit him too hard?

The cabin door flies open, but the movement barely registers in the corner of my eye. I haul Allen away from the wall, and he grunts. The halo returns full force, almost blinding.

Good. He's okay.

Better than okay. He punches me in the gut and goes for the gun again.

Playing possum must be how he's gotten through life and gone undetected. Pretending to be a harmless, nonthreatening guy. Not this time. Halo or no halo, this guy has brought enough death to the world.

As his hand closes over the gun handle again, he takes a quick glance up. What he sees behind me distracts him for a split second. Long enough for me to wrench his wrist sideways.

The gun goes off again, a loud bang in my ears.

Another scream follows. Sounds like Ivory again. But there's no time to figure out if anyone was hit.

Allen puts one of his bony knees in my chest and shoves, attempting to dislodge my hold on his wrist. I can't overcome his leverage. Plus, the move is pressing enough on my lungs to limit my air supply.

With his other hand, he slams a fist into my right side—the side with my still-healing bayonet wound. Pain knifes through my abdomen.

A menacing growl comes from near my left ear. Has Pepper turned on me now that I'm wrestling with his master? I can't break my focus to find out.

A furry shape darts around me.

Allen lets out a growl of his own, then yelps in pain.

A mass of mottled black and brown and white fur has latched on to Allen's ankle, lips curled back, teeth digging in.

Daisy?

He lowers his leg from my chest to kick at her.

I elbow him in the gut, and he clenches. He tries to curl into a ball, but Daisy won't let go of his ankle.

"Stop!" he yells.

The gun is still in his hand, and I still have his wrist in a vise-grip. We are in a stalemate, but the angle of the barrel keeps moving randomly as he thrashes around.

"Brenda, do something!" Rasher yells from behind.

Footsteps clomp over my shoulder. In a quiet voice that sounds nothing like the assertive Ranger Brenda Morrow I've come to know, she says, "Drop the gun."

Allen looks up at her with pleading eyes. Perhaps asking her to get the dog off him. Without a word, he complies by letting go of the gun.

I scoop it up and scoot backward, making sure not to get between Morrow's gun and Allen. He's still groaning from the pain Daisy is inflicting, and Morrow isn't doing anything except standing there.

When I'm a few feet away from them, I flip around to kneel on the ground and whistle. "Daisy, come here. Good girl."

She lets go of Allen's leg and trots over like chomping on a serial killer is part of a normal doggie playdate. I rub the scruff behind her ears. "You did so good."

"Mars, help me find some rope, please," Rasher says.

Ah, park rangers might have guns for protection, but in this day and age, they don't have much need for handcuffs. As I stand, my gaze falls on a man wearing a flannel jacket and back-pack who is blocking the door to the cabin. Gerald Morgan.

Suspicion wriggles through my gut. "What's he doing here?"

Morrow answers, "I ran into him on the way up. He said he wanted to help."

A Good Samaritan? Or trying to insert himself so he could control the outcome? Is his *help* going to be helping Allen escape?

In a rush, Gerald swings his backpack off his shoulder, crouches down, and begins to dig around in it. Maybe searching for a weapon. I tense and take a step toward him. Then, his fist comes out clutching a ball of twine.

"Oh, great." I hold my hand out, but Gerald doesn't give me the ball.

Instead, he leaves his pack and heads for Allen while unrolling the twine. When he gets close, he barks, "Roll over, Lund."

Allen glares at him briefly, then his gaze goes to Morrow. The gun seems to convince him to cooperate.

He rolls to his stomach but keeps both hands under his torso. His hips move back and forth as he shuffles around. What is he doing?

Gerald moves to grab his right wrist.

Allen's left hand shifts down. He's getting something from his pocket.

"Look out!" I yell just as Allen flips back over.

Allen's hand, brandishing a set of keys, arcs toward Gerald's stomach. A quick slice. Blood darkens the tail of his shirt. Allen must have some sort of sharp implement on his keychain.

Gerald leaps backward, holding the middle of his stomach.

"Drop it or I'll shoot!" Morrow yells.

From on his knees, he looks up at her like he's considering his options. She firms her jaw and tightens her grip on the weapon.

"Okay." Allen places the deadly implement on the floor. One of the keychains looks like a small switchblade.

"Shove them toward me," she demands.

He complies with a scowl, sending the keys on a vigorous bumpy slide. They slam into the baseboard on the wall behind Morrow.

As she bends to retrieve them, I grab the discarded ball of twine and cautiously approach Allen. What he doesn't know is that I have experience hog-tying an armadillo. That's how I managed to get my rescued armadillo Artie to the vet in my home time period.

I loop the twine around his left wrist first, then I use a kick to his hip to roll him over. A knee in the back arches him backward so I can swipe his other arm around and tie his wrists together with his feet.

One hog-tied serial killer as a very early Christmas present for the sheriff. He's only missing a bow around his neck.

His halo persists, though it has dimmed from earlier.

My satisfied smirk falls flat when I turn around. Rasher, Gerald, and Ivory all need something to stop the blood leaking from their bodies.

I grab a hand towel that is resting on the kitchen counter, crouch down, and press it into Gerald's stomach. He buttons his flannel coat over it to keep it in place.

Rasher has tied his black tie around his arm, but blood still seeps from his wound.

A sob comes from behind the chair. Morrow holsters her gun and goes to grab something from a lower cabinet—a first aid kit. In seconds, she has gauze wrapped around Ivory's neck.

As I stand from my crouch, I experience a rush of exhaustion. But there's no time to take a breather. We have three injured people and a serial killer to get off this mountain.

CHAPTER 16

Three ATVs are available, but only two drivers since everyone else is either injured or tied up. I've released Allen's legs to allow him to sit on the vehicle, while keeping his wrists tied. When I propose that Ranger Morrow drive Ivory and Rasher to get help while I drive Gerald and tied-up Allen, she flat-out refuses.

"You're still a suspect in the killings. For all I know, you're this man's accomplice and you just put on a good show of capturing him. As a park official, I will take responsibility for him."

"But what if he tries to fight on the way?"

She gives me a look that says I'm the most sexist man she's ever met to question her abilities. "Who just came to save you?" She jerks a thumb at Allen. "I can handle it. What choice do we have? They're too injured to stay up here for the night."

She has a point.

"Besides, I want Rasher to stay with you. To keep an eye on you."

She gets on her ATV, and I guide Allen to sit on the back. With his hands bound behind him, he will have to squeeze his legs to keep from falling off. That should keep him from causing trouble, as long as Morrow doesn't stop anywhere. Gerald climbs on the back behind Allen and wraps an arm around the man. Gerald gives me a nod as if to say he's got this.

She revs the vehicle, then turns to me. "It's faster to return to the Sula Ranger Station to call the police. My ATV has more horsepower, so I'll go on ahead. That way, I can have the ambulance waiting when you get there."

"Okay. Be careful."

After she leaves, I climb on the front of the ATV Rasher and I brought from Allen's house. We place Ivory in the middle with Rasher securing her from the back. She has lost a lot of blood, and her scared eyes are at half mast. We've got to get her to a hospital.

The ATV lurches forward. I do my best to stay on what looks like the path lit by the one headlight on the front. I'm trusting Rasher to slap me if I stray in the wrong direction.

It certainly cools down at night in the mountains. Ordinarily, I'd be shivering as the cooler air rushes past us, but the press of the two bodies behind me and the near-constant flow of adrenaline keeps me warm.

Pepper and Daisy are running loose to make their own way wherever they choose. I didn't see where Pepper went, but Daisy took off into the woods ahead of us.

We travel for an hour in silence. The wind rushes by my ears. My body is pounded by the bumps in the trail and then the crush of the bodies behind as I rebound from the bumps. At least, Ivory's grip around my waist stays strong.

Suddenly, Rasher calls out, "What's that?"

I slow the vehicle, then come to a complete stop. The trail—really just dirt depressions worn into the landscape—sits on a small rise approximately six feet above a clearing. Scrub brush and weeds are flattened at the side of the trail as if a vehicle traveled in that direction.

I climb off the ATV to check it out. My distance vision is

limited to only about thirty feet out into the night, but two dark stripes seem to cut through the other foliage in the clearing. Rasher comes to stand beside me.

"ATV tracks?" I ask.

He nods solemnly. "Brenda must have gone off trail. She righted herself, so let's hope they all made it back to the station."

The sound of a wolf's bay makes the hair on the back of my neck stand up. Another reason not to linger.

We climb back on, and I double my speed. I shouldn't have let her go with Allen. She has his preferred hair color. And she's from this area. For all I know, she's the one who started his obsession.

"Does Allen know Ranger Morrow?" I yell over the noise of the engine.

He leans over Ivory to reply. "Not specifically. Just the way we all know each other in Meadowlark."

Could Allen have loved her from afar and started this whole killing spree to get her attention? That would explain why the killing ground is so close to the ranger's station. It could even explain why he cuts the women's throats, almost like he's drawing the cravat that Morrow wears as part of her uniform. But this theory doesn't explain the young girls or the scrunchies. Unless he knew Morrow from childhood and is fixated on both versions of her?

If any of these thoughts are true, then I just left her with the one person who is obsessed with her. Tied up or not, he could be desperate enough to try anything to get to her. Would Gerald be able to help?

As we approach the ranger's station half an hour later, the situation is better than I feared. Morrow stands unharmed next to her empty ATV. But where is Allen? And Gerald?

I pull to a stop, and Rasher jumps off. "Lund has escaped?"

She nods while straightening the headlight on her vehicle. "He caused me to veer off the road, then he ran off. And worse yet. I can't get the radio to work to call for an ambulance or backup. See if you guys can get it working while I go after the prisoner."

Rasher grabs the handle bars with his good arm and looks her in the eye. "Not alone. Where's Gerald?"

"After the accident, he ran off into the woods."

"Why would he do that?"

"Who knows? Maybe he was afraid of Lund. Maybe he's working with Lund. I'll look for him while searching for the prisoner. Get inside. You need medical attention." She sweeps a hand at Ivory who still sits on the ATV as if dazed. "Plus, you're responsible for her safety. Get the radio working or take my truck to the hospital. You can send troopers as backup once you get in contact with someone."

Still, Rasher hesitates.

"I can't let him just get away," Morrow insists.

"I'll go with her," I say.

Morrow shakes her head. "No. I don't trust you."

She looks like she wants to leave without any more discussion, but Rasher continues to hold on to her handlebars and block her path. "I trust him."

"Why?"

Rasher has his back to me, so I can't see his face, but he takes a few beats to answer. Almost as if he doesn't know why he trusts me.

Finally, he says, "Mars may have started at the wrong place at the wrong time, but everything he's done since then has been exactly what I'd do in this situation. And going off alone against a killer is not smart."

"Fine. We're wasting time arguing." She glares at me. "Get on."

I give her a sheepish look. "How about I drive? My ATV isn't damaged."

"Technically, it's a stolen ATV, but whatever. Yours is in better shape right now."

While she gets on the back of my vehicle, I sneak a look at my phone. The display says 4:29 a.m. A quick adjustment based on what I guessed the time to be earlier gives me a time close to 10:30 p.m. in this time period. Not quite three hours before I return home. Assuming I return.

I'm forced to stuff the phone in my front pocket so Morrow doesn't see it. Then, I rev the engine and take off toward the area where she lost Allen.

Going mostly uphill is slower, so it takes an hour to get back to the crash site. I park the ATV just off the trail.

Morrow hops off and draws her gun. She's a lefty. I hadn't noticed in the cabin. I watch over her shoulder as she inspects the ground. She identifies a few footprints heading into the surrounding trees.

Before pursuing them, she straightens and turns to face me, gun angled down. "I'm putting my life in your hands, and I don't even know your last name."

That's probably true. I've told Rasher, but not her. "I'm Mars Lockporte." At her wide-eyed look, I rush to add, "From Colorado."

"Do you have family from Idaho?"

"Yes, how did you …" Then, I understand her shocked expression and why her name had sounded familiar. "You're a Lockporte."

"That's my father's name. I go by my mother's maiden name." She puts one hand on her hip and mutters, "Huh."

"Well"—I gesture in the direction of the footprints—"shall we?"

A quick nod. She raises her gun and enters the forest.

I follow behind while mulling this discovery over. I've finally found the connection, the convergence of Lockporte and Millstone DNA. I've done everything I can to make sure Ivory survives. Hopefully, that will bring Liam back in my time. And now I've found the reason why I connected with Morrow. But why this killer? Why Allen? And what does the halo truly mean?

Did I save him just to have him escape and keep killing? Perhaps there's still something else going on here that I don't understand. Or maybe I'm merely trying to bring meaning out of the random event of being literally dropped into a murder mystery.

CHAPTER 17

WE FOLLOW Allen's trail in the dark for hours, using Ranger Morrow's flashlight in the tree cover and moonlight in the clearings. She's a good tracker, spotting every half print and broken twig.

I didn't think to borrow Rasher's jacket before we left, but the exertion of the hunt keeps the cold at bay, even with my short sleeves. Every rustling leaf blowing in the wind sets my nerves on edge. More deadly beasts than just Allen prowl out here. Though he is our biggest concern.

Is he hiding behind a tree waiting to ambush us? Or is he attempting to get as far away from Meadowlark as possible? At the moment, only four people know he's the killer, but even if he kills Morrow and myself tonight, he'd still have to hunt down and kill Rasher and Ivory, and possibly even Gerald, before they tell the authorities. His secret will get out. The smart move is to run.

"What happened?" Morrow points to my right side.

A quarter-sized stain darkens the fabric. My bayonet wound must have split open. I groan. "A scratch, I guess. Rasher will want to kill me for ruining his prized T-shirt."

She laughs. "You've gotten to know him well in such a short amount of time."

I shrug and continue walking. She shifts direction ahead of me, following clues I wouldn't have any hope of finding in the dark.

The longer we search, the more uncomfortable I become with being unarmed. In hindsight, I should have taken Rasher's gun with me, though Morrow surely would have objected. I pick up a stick about the length and width of a baseball bat. Morrow turns and squints at me. She's probably rolling her eyes, but it's too dark to tell.

We are deep into the wilderness now. My only consolation is that while following Allen's trail, we must be leaving an even bigger trail for the authorities to follow. But will they come right away or wait until morning?

The hauntingly deep howl of a wolf sounds again, sending chills down my arms. Morrow stops to assess where it's coming from, cocking her head to and fro. The echoes of the cry swirl around us.

She appears to believe the howl is coming from the north because she points in that direction. To my surprise, she heads toward the wolf. Maybe she thinks Allen disturbed the wolf's lair, and we will find him there.

More surprising still, after a few paces, she gives me a wink and says, "Wildlife gives you a wider berth if you talk to them." Then, she throws her head back and lets her own howl loose.

I freeze on the spot. The higher-pitched tone of her cry strikes a chord in my memory.

She notices that I've stopped and gestures for me to follow. My feet trod slowly behind her while my mind spins at a breakneck pace.

That same howl in that same pitch echoed through the forest the night I arrived. Slipping between the leaves. Reaching my ears just before the killer disappeared, as if he was following the sound.

It wasn't a wolf. It was *her*.

A paradigm shifts in my mind a hundred and eighty degrees. Ranger Brenda Morrow works close to the killing ground. She's comfortable in these woods. She would know about the old ranger's station since she was the one to routinely check on it. She could get access to Rasher's diabetes medication to set him up for Serenity's murder.

I suck in a sharp breath as the final piece clicks into place: When we were leaving, she said it was faster to go back to the Sula Ranger Station than to go back to Allen's house. She was right because even though Rasher and I got to the cabin quicker than she did, the terrain going that way is steeper and would be more difficult while transporting injured people. But Rasher never told her where we were coming from. How did she know where Allen lives if they barely know each other?

Two different victim profiles.

Two different styles of killing.

Two killers.

Turns out my twenty-first-century knowledge of serial killers has also put blinders on my eyes. Most serial killers are men. *Most.*

She is Allen's partner, or maybe even the mastermind of the whole set of murders. Adrenaline floods my brain, sending my heart rate soaring as my predicament becomes clear.

I'm alone in the woods with two killers who are searching for each other.

CHAPTER 18

WHAT WOULD my crime junkie sister do? Probably try to trap Morrow into a confession and record it. But I can't record anything on my phone because then I'd have to explain to the police what kind of device my phone is. Plus, I don't have time to get a recording to the police. It must be around twelve thirty or one o'clock. With any luck, I'll be leaving soon.

Maybe that's my solution. Keep her and Allen busy until I leap out. But then what? No one else knows she's involved. Rasher will send the police after Allen, and she'll get away with it all. Assuming she doesn't point the blame at Rasher for Serenity's death.

This pondering leads me to another burning question: Is she going to reunite with Allen to run away with him or to tie up loose ends? She might plan to shoot him before he can implicate her. That would be best-case scenario for me, as long as she still believes I have no idea of her guilt. But if they are planning to run away together, they would want to eliminate me as a witness.

I need to get her talking to find out where her intentions lie. Best to come off as guileless as possible. I softly tap her arm. "I have to confess something about my family. I left home to get away from my dad." I'm playing the runaway hippie, but wanting to get away from my father isn't an exaggeration. "Since you're a Lockporte, I'd like to know what your home was like growing up."

"You want to do this now?" she hisses.

"Things might get crazy when we find Allen, so why not now?"

She pauses, looking down at the leaves scattered on the forest floor. Maybe it's the reminder that we're related that causes her to hesitate. How would she explain my death to her relatives? "Fine, my family history in ten seconds. My parents divorced when I was ten. I was energetic and rambunctious. Too much so for them. My dad was the one to leave. I never spoke to him again. My mother died of lung cancer a year ago. Now, let's get on with this."

Morrow returns her focus to Allen's trail while I ponder her words. Her mother died a year ago. Was that the catalyst for acting on her murderous impulses? She seems to have blamed herself for the divorce. But her sister disappeared when she was younger, according to Rasher. Both events had to be traumatic.

So, if Allen is the throat slasher, as evidenced by Ivory's injuries, then Morrow would be the strangler of little girls. Why? Perhaps she hated herself as a little girl? No matter her twisted motives, what she's done is inexcusable ... and I'm related to her.

If I could look inside my soul right now, it would resemble a wilted piece of lettuce. What does it say about me and my genetics that my family tree is full of serial killers and conmen? But then, I remember the Civil War soldier I shot and almost killed. The one who looked like me but didn't kill me when he could have finished me off. Maybe my obsession with genealogy research has blinded me to the power we all hold, a power greater than the leverage of our DNA—the power of choice.

My long-dead ancestors have made their choices, good or bad. I need to put those aside and determine my own destiny.

Even if no one but me knows it, my legacy will be to take Brenda Morrow out. As my cousin Rochelle would say, *When part of the family tree rots, it's time to cut off the branch.*

To that end, it would be better to confront her before she meets up with Allen, rather than face them both together. Maybe I could hit her before she turns around. I raise the stick inch by inch until it's level with my bicep. As soon as I pull it back to wind up, she glances over her shoulder, so I have to quickly act casual.

Her scowl says she's not buying it.

While the gun is still pointing at the ground, I ask a question to throw her off. "How did you and Allen get together?"

She furrows her brow, but her eyes are in shadow. "What do you mean?"

I swing the stick, not at her head or the trunk of her body, but at her gun hand, just as she begins to raise it.

A sickening crunch. The gun drops, falling on a pile of leaves.

I throw the stick to the side to go for the gun, but before I can reach it, she drops her flashlight and snatches the gun up with her right hand.

The paltry light from the flashlight on the ground throws dancing shadows around us as she shakes her head in a pitying way. "Compassionate play, not going for the head." A grin splits her face. "Unfortunately for you, I'm ambidextrous."

That's one thing we have in common. Maybe it's a strong Lockporte trait.

She backs away from me a few steps and throws her pack to the ground. Through the partially open zipper, I see a saffron yellow scrunchie sitting right on top. While holding the weapon under her armpit, she slips the scrunchie on her left wrist and doubles it up to put pressure on her injury.

I lunge for her while she's distracted, but she's half a step too far from me.

Before I can reach her, she has the gun trained on me once again. "Don't move."

Maybe I can talk my way out of this. "Why the kids, Brenda?"

My use of her first name seems to throw her. Or maybe there's some small remorse buried deep down. *Way* deep down.

"How did you know?" she asks.

"I heard your fake wolf cry in the woods last night."

She blinks a few times as her gaze clouds over. But then, a microsecond later, she focuses vulture-sharp eyes on me. "I'm not evil. They were kids who either had no one to care for them or who were being abused. I saved them from living a hard life."

The weak justification for murder makes me sick but doesn't surprise me. Other than self-defense or defense of another, there is no justification for murder. But feeding into her aggrandizement is my best chance to figure out a way to stop her from shooting me. "So, you saved them because no one saved you?"

"Don't patronize me."

I take a slow step closer. "I really want to understand."

That part isn't a lie. I've always sought—and failed—to understand criminal behavior. My dad is the perfect example. What makes him believe his needs and desires rank above other people's? In his opinion, he's only doing what other people would do by looking out for himself. He claims he's just better at it than other people. But in my opinion, his obsession with control is like a monster that constantly must be fed.

Is that what it's like for Morrow?

Most female serial killers kill for money. As a female killer who kills for a different reason, she is the unicorn of unicorns. Maybe she'll tell me her reasons.

I prod her a little. "If I'm related to a killer, I deserve to know why she's done the things she's done."

Her feet shuffle backward. Despite her boast, she doesn't seem confident with the gun in her right hand. It sways slightly as she tries to keep it trained on me.

"You deserve?" She pushes her shoulders back. "I don't owe you anything. The Lockportes haven't done me any favors.

Before he left, my father was a bully. My mom never stood up to him."

I've got her riled up now. Who knows if that's good for me or not. "He hit you?"

"Nothing so bold. Just did everything he could to let me know that I didn't come out right. I acted more like a son than a daughter. Cross your legs, Brenda. Wear a dress, Brenda. Don't go out without makeup, Brenda. He thought I was only good for catching a man's attention. And I didn't get any attention from him unless I acted *feminine*. Finally, when I wouldn't conform, he took all my trousers and burned them in the backyard fire pit."

I take another step closer, though I don't exactly have a plan. "That wasn't fair. What kind of man shames his daughter for being a tomboy?"

"Except for Allen, every single man I've ever met shames women. They all want to keep a woman under their thumbs."

She *is* doing the same thing as my dad—grappling for control. Even excusing a man like Allen, who takes the ultimate control over women's lives. Wait, unless she's the dominant one, meaning Allen does what he does to please her.

"Every single man, Brenda?" The deep voice cuts through the tension like a laser through a thick fog.

Rasher. How is he here? He was supposed to go to the hospital with Ivory. He flips on a flashlight and steps out from behind a tree with a bandage wrapped around his arm on the outside of his coat. His gun is trained on Morrow. Instinctively, I shuffle a few steps closer to him.

"I treated you like my boss," he says. "I gave you respect."

Her confident façade falters, then she rallies with a fiery retort. "Not enough to follow my directions, apparently."

Rasher tilts his head as if disappointed in her answer. "The radio system was unplugged. You should have easily figured out the problem. That's how I knew you did it to delay us getting help. I had to ask myself why."

She rolls her eyes. "Ivory?"

"On her way to the hospital. The ambulance drivers have my verbal report, and they know I came after you. It's time to give this up, Brenda."

"What is Ivory going to tell them? That I didn't realize the radio was unplugged. I can control that narrative."

She's implying Rasher and I won't be around to tell them any different. Which is why she isn't trying to convince him of her innocence. But alarm bells are ringing in my head. She's sounding too confident with Rasher holding a gun on her.

I glance behind me. The halo gives him away, though it would be too dark to see him otherwise. Allen creeps up on Rasher's position with something in his hand. My baseball-bat branch?

Rasher reads my concern and turns, his finger sliding over the trigger.

Not again.

I can't let him shoot Allen. Even as I dive at Rasher, my brain questions what I'm doing. Why do I have this unreasonable desire to protect a killer, even when he's about to hurt me or Rasher? It must be the halo. We are tied to each other in this leap in the same way Long and I were tied to each other in my first leap.

My arms close around Rasher, and I shove him to the ground. With a grunt, I land on top of him.

Rasher's shot goes wide, as does Allen's baseball swing.

No one is hurt, but Rasher and I are not in an enviable position. Morrow stalks over to stand above us. She cocks her gun and points it at my head.

CHAPTER 19

"Why did you do that?" Morrow asks me.

I turn apologetic eyes to Rasher. "I wish I knew."

"Maybe it's because of the aura," Allen says from beside her.

They both stare down at me like I'm an unknown species of insect, which they are equally as likely to either document my characteristics or step on me.

"Seriously," she says, "this is the guy you told me about? The one you've been afraid of?"

He bristles. "Not afraid. I'm being cautious. Can you explain what I'm seeing?"

"No, because nothing is there. Maybe you're losing it."

Allen looks offended but doesn't say a word in his own defense as he bends to pick up a flashlight. I may be right about Morrow being the dominant partner.

Rasher glares at me, for good reason. This isn't like the last time where I was protecting him from a knife throw. He had enough time to take Allen out before Allen could strike. He's questioning anew whose side I'm on.

Allen crouches down to look me in the eye. "Why did you just save me?"

"I'm not sure," I repeat with a sigh. "The halo feels like a bond I can't break or let someone else break. I've been racking my brain trying to figure out how you ended up with the halo. To figure out why you would deserve to live."

My bluntness seems to hit Allen hard. He pulls back and stands. His eyes drop to the ground, and his lower lip trembles. Does he regret the things he's done?

I open my mouth to push him a little, but Rasher puts a staying hand on my arm. His anger had turned to confusion at the talk of halos, but now, he raises his brows like he's just figured something out or like he's scheming something.

"Allen," Rasher begins in a soothing voice I've not heard him use, "think about this from a heavenly perspective. Maybe there's something you need to clear off your conscience. I believe you were saved by the guy with the halo so that you can bring closure to what happened long ago." He throws a pointed look at Morrow. "Brenda's sister, the one who chose to live with her father. She disappeared and was never found."

Rasher waits a beat, but Allen avoids eye contact and doesn't respond.

"Brenda was angry with her sister. That much I know."

Panic drenches both killers' faces. But then, Morrow's features relax. Perhaps it doesn't matter to her if Allen tells us because she will just kill us anyway. She runs a hand over her hair, many strands of which have fallen out of her braids, but she winces from the injury to her hand. I take some satisfaction in that.

"Is this really necessary to discuss?" she asks Allen.

He stays silent as he circles around her and crouches close to me again. With one finger, he reaches out and touches the outside of my bare elbow.

"You can't feel the halo," I tell him. "It's quantum in nature."

"What?"

"Quantum … uh … never mind."

He shakes his head as if he's trying to shake off the effects of the halo. I can relate. For the last twenty hours, my anger at what he's done has unhappily coexisted with my need to protect him. This doesn't make any sense.

Yet, I still try to work it out too. If I'm guessing correctly that they weren't held responsible for their crimes in the original timeline, then maybe I'm supposed to keep him alive long enough to see justice. Or maybe Rasher is on the right track and Allen is supposed to tell what he knows.

"Brenda's sister …" I start.

"Pamela," Rasher supplies.

"Pamela didn't run away, did she?" I ask Allen.

His gray eyes focus on me without blinking, as if he can't look away. "Some say so."

I don't have to ask what people assumed happened to her. In any disappearance, the father would be the primary suspect. No one would look twice at her sweet older sister, especially if she wasn't living with them. I give Allen a subtle nod, telling him it's okay to let it out.

He sucks in a shallow breath, then releases it little by little. But I'm not the one he needs permission from. A quick glance at Morrow over his shoulder. She rolls her eyes again like this is no more of an inconvenience than waiting her turn at the DMV.

The words tumble out of him in a rush as he stands. "Brenda had a friend pass Pamela a note on her way to school that said she wanted to mend their relationship. That she didn't blame Pamela for choosing their father. The note asked her to meet Brenda later that night at an old barn but to be sure not to tell their father. Brenda said she didn't want to see him."

My voice cracks as I force the next words out. "How did she … die?"

"Same as the other young ones. Strangled."

So, Morrow is the one who killed the kids. "How old was Pamela?"

His voice goes into a lower register. "Nine."

Even Allen doesn't understand Morrow's compulsion to kill little girls. But I do. At least in the clinical sense. She's acting out over and over again the worst thing she's ever done. Driven by guilt and anger. Whether it's anger at herself or lingering anger at her father—and her sister for siding with him—remains to be seen.

"I've asked her why the kids." He swivels to face her. "Right, B.? I've asked, but you never answer."

"It's an insult to ask." Her voice is gravelly. "I've never asked why you do it."

"Because you know why. It's for you."

My mouth goes dry. Not due to his disturbing words, but because the halo has disappeared, blinking out as if it was never there.

It blinks on again for a fraction of a second, a flash of brilliance lighting up his form, then it disappears again. His outline goes dark.

Morrow's eyebrows draw together to scowl at him. "You were killing before I came along."

"Only once. When I told you, it impressed you so much that I kept going. I needed you to see me as strong, powerful, in control."

Doesn't seem like that worked out for him. Morrow has always had the control without him even realizing it. My father conned people in the same way. By making them think they were willingly doing the things he wanted.

In her distraction, Morrow's gun hand has lowered to point at my feet. Come to think of it, the gun has mostly been pointing at me, not often at Rasher. It must be easier to think about killing me, whom she's known for not quite a day, than to think about killing Rasher, whom she's worked with for years. Though undoubtedly, she's willing to kill us both eventually.

"Do you think I'm an imbecile?" she asks in a haughty tone. "Those women were substitutes. In killing them, you were trying to take control of *me*."

"No." He shakes his head sadly. "I killed every woman who caught my wandering eye who wasn't you."

A glint of truth radiates from his earnest gaze. In his view, he killed eleven women to keep himself faithful to one. A twisted love story. One that will not have a happily ever after.

"Do you mind if Mars and I just go while you two unpack all your baggage?" Rasher asks.

I could clap him on the back and say *Good one*, except drawing Morrow's attention to us probably wasn't the best idea in this situation. Unless he has a plan.

He squeezes my elbow and gives a slight nod to the right. His gun rests a few feet away. Allen never picked it up. Rasher is asking for a distraction, and I have just the thing.

I let out a dramatic breath. "It's over, Brenda. You can't kill us because I'm an undercover policeman."

I twist my left arm to expose my implant and tap it to fully turn the display on. The personal AI must be confused by this situation since it flashes between deep violet and periwinkle. Definitely high risk, which brings in the dark red, but it can't seem to decide whether to mix that with light blue for high reward or navy for low reward. Yeah, I get it.

I square my shoulders, daring her to contradict me. "We don't wear wires anymore. This is a recording device that's implanted in my skin. Your confession is all I needed."

Her injured hand comes to her hip. "And just how will you get the recording off that device?"

I dig my phone out of my front pocket. "I plug it into this."

She grabs the phone, wincing in pain from twisting her wrist. The movement turns the phone on. The icons lighting up my lock screen cause her to blink repeatedly at the brightness. Weather from a day eighty years in the future. A reminder of my father's parole hearing. And likely most confusing to her, my quantum wave detector app, which pings with a notification.

She flips the phone around to face me before realizing there's nothing on the back. In an instant, the time and app data register in my mind, driving me to interesting conclusions. Measuring quantum waves is not an exact process. The app measures background quantum waves at a relative arbitrary value of fifty percent, indicating an average number of quantum wave phenomena. The app is programmed to alert when the percentage gets higher than seventy-five, meaning several quantum waves are superimposed upon each other. Now, it's registering a level of ninety percent. That's odd enough on its own, but to have elevated levels when I leaped to this time period and again at 1:07, ten minutes before I'm supposed to leap out? That's too much of a coincidence.

But this scientific breakthrough, confirming that superimposed quantum waves help me travel, doesn't help keep me alive. Or Rasher, who is currently kneeling on my right and trying to edge toward his gun.

Allen points to my phone. "I saw that on him earlier."

"So, if I destroy this," Brenda says, "then no recording."

"Not true. They can still get the recording out of my elbow. Face it, there's no going back to your normal life."

She snorts. "I've never had a normal life."

Her intentions finally become crystal clear. She doesn't plan to blame this all on Allen so she can go back to business as usual. She has always planned to disappear once the collection of bodies were found. Let the police assume she's another victim.

Do her plans include Allen, though?

A hard glint comes into her eyes. "Guess I'll just have to kill you and cut the recording out."

CHAPTER 20

Now what? All I've done is give the two serial killers more reason to kill me. To kill *us*. I might be able to keep Morrow talking long enough to leap out, but that would leave Rasher to fend for himself against the two of them. I can't do that to him.

Which means I have to buy more time. "What happened to Gerald? If you don't mind me asking."

Morrow hands the phone off to Allen. He handles it with his fingertips, like it might electrocute him. It's still strange to look at him without the halo. Thank goodness the desire to protect him also seems to have disappeared.

A sideways smile crosses Allen's face. "I used Brenda's utility knife on him. We didn't want you to hear a shot."

His boast turns my stomach into an acid bath. Poor guy.

I'll have to try a different strategy. Maybe I can pit the killers against each other. I ignore Morrow completely, knowing it will gall her, and focus on Allen. "I think you've done all the legwork for this killing project. Why doesn't she give you any credit?"

A few seconds of silence pass as Allen blinks repeatedly, first at me, then at Morrow. She is clearly the one in charge, but what's not clear is whether that's because he has no spine or because he's in love with her.

"Why are you looking at her? Can't you speak for yourself?"

His gaze swings back to me, now full of anger. "I think my work speaks for itself."

"Not the little girls. That wasn't your work at all."

He rubs a toe in the carpet of leaves.

From the corner of my eye, I see Rasher inching closer to the weapon. I have to keep their focus on me. "How did you get them for her?"

His voice is so quiet, I barely catch the name when he speaks it. "Pepper."

Of course. He used the dog to lure the girls close enough to grab.

He glances at me again, and his eyes widen slightly. Does he still see a halo on me? Or is he picking up on all the quantum wave activity surrounding us?

"I told them he was a service dog, that he would pick things up for me because I have a bad back. They always wanted to pet him."

"That's how you got them in your car."

He scrunches his face. "They were lost little girls."

"They might have been lost, but somebody cared about them. Loved them." Time to see what kind of conscience he has inside, if any. "Why did you get them for her? Why did you let her turn you into a monster?"

I might have gone too far with the last question, especially since he was likely a monster before he met Morrow. He shutters his gaze and turns his back to me.

Morrow grins while looking straight into my eyes. She knows what I'm trying to do and that it likely won't work. Her control over Allen is as solid as the mountain I'm sitting on.

Still, I can't give up. I direct my next words to her, surprised by what comes out. "There's something else you should know."

This is a last ditch effort. Even as I say the words, I beg my brain to come up with something more helpful. Nothing surfaces except the thought of taking drastic measures against her. If

Allen decides not to protect her, I may have a chance. But then, a vital warning rises in my brain. I might be directly related to Brenda Morrow. If I end her life early, I could be blinking myself out of existence.

An image of Torri swims in my head, dark hair blowing across her shoulders, a half smile on her lips. She would never know I existed. Never miss me. And of course, I wouldn't be around to miss her. So why does the thought of never seeing her again hit like a brick slamming into my head?

Then, my mind's eye switches to Long's grateful face after I saved him from the hanging tree—a tree he'd been willing to die on to save me. A tree he probably died on in the original timeline before I saved him. I will take his sacrificial example to heart. That is the man I want to be. Not a man like my father.

Though I'm not controlled or patient, I can emulate Long's sacrifice in my own way. I can use my brains, my recklessness, and my impulsivity to stop Morrow, no matter the consequences to my future life.

This is the 1970s, after all. An age of limited communications. She can't know everything, especially how good I am at bluffing.

At my continued hesitation, she gives me a condescending smile. Her words drip with sarcasm. "Tell me, Mars Lockporte, what is it that I have to know right now before you die? What do you think you can say that will keep me from shooting you?"

I fix her with a hard gaze. "It's not just Ivory you have to worry about. You're forgetting there is one more person who can identify you."

She points with the barrel of the gun first at Rasher. "One." Then at me. "Two. Nope, don't seem to be missing anyone."

This rests on the assumption she's been in on Allen's kills. It's a chance worth taking. I lean forward, coming to my knees with my forehead perilously close to the gun barrel. "Okay, then. Go ahead and do it."

She leans back on her heels. The implications are running

through her mind. She's a lot smarter than most people give her credit for—myself included. A sarcastic comment is on the tip of my tongue, *Nothing worse than a smart serial killer*, but I push down my coping mechanism in favor of waiting her out.

Ten seconds later, she shifts forward again and smacks the side of the gun across my cheek. "Who do you mean?"

My neck snaps back from the hit. But she's not that strong. I feign a cry of pain before scowling at her.

She rears back again, and I bite out the name as if reluctant. "Serenity Brooks."

Confusion wrinkles her pale features. "She's dead."

"Not hardly. That's just what we wanted the killer to think."

When I leaped here, Allen was already out in the woods. I thought he was dumping a body, but he must have been looking for Serenity. In the original timeline, I wouldn't have been here to find her, yet she still would have ended up at the ranger's station. If Rasher had found her, he might have called Morrow first since she is his supervisor and would be closer than the ambulance. Chances are good that Morrow originally killed them both at the ranger's station. Perhaps this is why I leaped here, to change things.

Morrow's sharp gaze skewers Allen.

He puts his hands in the air. "I gave her all the insulin you provided. It should have been enough to kill her." He tilts his head. "After I took Ivory, I went back to check. All the police officers were investigating, and one of the nurses confirmed she was dead. He has to be bluffing."

"How can you be sure?" she asks.

"Well, they had a sheet over her, but the room was locked down. I couldn't get in to see the body."

Morrow lets out a long sigh as if it pains her to have to deal with incompetence. Then, she shrugs. "Ivory doesn't know anything useful. And Serenity can't identify *me*."

With her gaze fixed on mine, she quickly raises her right

hand to point the weapon at Allen. Her eyes squint down a bit as she turns her head a fraction to aim, but she doesn't say another word as she squeezes the trigger.

CHAPTER 21

THE BLAST KNOCKS Allen backward into a tree. Bits of bark go flying. A small hole opens in his chest. Oddly, his expression isn't one of shock or fear. He appears resigned, as if he deserves this fate. Maybe he does.

Ever since the halo disappeared, after he told us about Pamela, his outline has been solid and dark. Now, the light in his eyes begins to fade. His last words are rough whispers. "Pam … woods … barn."

The location doesn't mean anything to me, but maybe it does to Rasher. Morrow turns away from the man she just murdered, and I catch her signature eye roll.

"He always did talk too much," she says.

Not far from me, Rasher tenses. We're running out of time. He's going to make a move.

I rush to distract her again. "I think I understand that the other kids stemmed from what you did to your sister, but why kill her in the first place? Just because you were angry?"

"Don't pity Pamela. She deserved to pay for her betrayal. She decided to live with my father because he promised her a house with a swimming pool." She snorted. "A pool. Such a worthwhile trade to give up half her family."

Such a stupid thing to kill someone over. But I can't say that. It would only enrage her.

In the woods, close to the tree where Allen has fallen, shuffling noises catch my attention. Something is rooting around. Then comes a familiar soulful howl.

"Daisy?" I call out.

No answering howl or bark, but more shuffling. Something is coming toward us through the trees. Hopefully it's her.

"Over here, girl!" Thank God that dog has been persistent in following me.

"Shut up!" Morrow says while swinging her arm back and forth from the trees to me.

Just as Daisy's mottled fur breaks through the foliage, Rasher leaps at Morrow, grabbing her arm and shoving the gun to point at the night sky.

She steps back to get away but is held in place by a tree trunk.

Rasher pins her wrist to the tree. With his other hand, he puts a forearm across her chest.

Daisy comes first to me, then quickly refocuses on the fighting people. She plants her feet and lets out a series of fierce growls, though it's unclear who her ire is directed at.

Rasher and Morrow struggle as she keeps a tight grip on the gun. She grunts when he slams her wrist into the tree bark several times.

Finally, the gun flies from her hand. Daisy jumps back as the weapon lands a few feet from my knees.

A tingling sensation starts at my fingertips and spreads up my arms. *No.* I fight against it to stay present. I can't leap out yet. Because I see what Rasher doesn't—the glint of steel from just under Morrow's shirt.

"Knife!" I yell.

The tingling grows until it feels like worms are crawling under my skin. The pain will come next, starting deep in my core. But I can't leave him in dire straits.

Before going for the blade, Morrow sweeps her elbow up and jabs Rasher in the Adam's apple. He coughs and sputters, sucking in ragged breaths, barely keeping his hands on her.

She grips the hilt of the knife with her left hand, despite the injury causing her to wince, and yanks it fully from her waistband. She doesn't need to aim much with a blade.

I scramble forward, grappling for the gun. The first thing within my reach ends up being my phone, which Allen dropped when Morrow shot him.

As my fingers close around it, my hand goes translucent. I can't pick it up. No way. I will *not* leave now.

I push internally at the hazy, dizzy feeling, banishing it to the edges of my consciousness. It recedes slightly, enough to allow me to grab the phone.

With a shaking hand, I press the flashlight button. As it did with Allen when I arrived, it surprises and blinds her. But this merely makes her hesitate. She doesn't drop the knife.

Daisy prances anxiously around the only weapon left near me—the gun. I don't want to kill Morrow, could possibly kill myself in the process, but I'm running out of options. If I don't do something immediately, I'll leap out and she will kill Rasher and escape, never to face justice for all she's done.

Like in my father's case, justice matters. The lives of those she killed matter. Rasher's life matters. No more working the situation to my benefit. It's time to do the right thing and let the consequences fall where they may.

Morrow draws her arm back, ready to strike. The knife blade still glints in the light from my phone, which I've thrown to the ground so I can go after the gun.

Leaves scatter as I lunge and scoop up the weapon. I twist my wrist to aim, but then I hesitate. Rasher's body is covering hers. The only thing sticking out is her leg from the thigh down. I'm not confident enough in my shooting skill to hit her leg in the dark.

She pushes against Rasher, probably to get a better angle to strike.

They move away from the trunk about six inches, but then, he slams her back against the tree trunk again using his forearm on her chest.

Her whole body shudders, but she still doesn't drop the knife.

A loud creak comes from the tree high above us. It sounds like it's originating from as high as heaven itself. We all look up.

Snap. Crack.

A dark shape about the size of a baseball plummets down.

Morrow shifts away from Rasher just as he shifts a few inches back. Half of her chest is exposed. Not enough for a shot.

A large pinecone hits Rasher on the top of the head with a solid *thunk*, stunning him. He sways a few more inches away from her.

She seizes the opportunity, rearing back to strike.

No time left. I have to chance it.

I line up on her chest and fire.

I'm a fraction of a second too late. She buries the knife in Rasher's chest just before she's thrown back by the force of the bullet.

Momentum slams her body into the side of the tree. She spins half a turn before landing on her side on the carpeting of leaves. Her face is turned away. Hopefully, she's dead.

Rasher clutches his chest with one hand, then steadies himself on the tree trunk with the other. He glances at Morrow briefly. Then, his gaze focuses on me.

His eyes widen in an owlish look.

The hazy feeling is coming back full force. Like my cells are morphing into the white static on a black-and-white television from this era.

I don't have much longer.

My phone shines up at me, a bright beacon on the leaf litter five feet away. If I leave it here, it could cause technological advances fifty years too early. What would that change in the future? I can't take the chance.

I struggle to keep myself intact while I dive forward.

My chest smacks the ground when I land, and my fingers brush something hard like plastic. I clamp my hand around it.

Then, the pain hits. I double over and clench as tiny knives seem to be cutting me apart from the inside. A low groan escapes my lips.

"Godspeed," I hear Rasher say as everything goes dark.

CHAPTER 22

University of Colorado Boulder
September 21, 2051
7:17 a.m.

I FALL to my knees on the gray tile of my office floor. Same position as after my first leap. Must be the strain on my body from quantum travel. Except this time, I'm clutching my phone in my hand, thank God.

Though I'm not in pain now, the memory of the pain reverberates through my mind like an echo. I shake it off and look around.

The room is empty.

Has it only been twenty-one hours since I left? Each of the two leaps I've taken have seemed to go on for a lifetime.

My screensaver flashes my home time—7:17 a.m. It also displays my running inspirational quote: *A leap in time requires a leap in logic.*

It's a quote from the draft of my doctoral thesis, but it was inspired by Dr. Pearce and his take on time travel. That is, traveling in time would seem as impossible to most people in this era as a weapons drone would seem to a musket-carrying Revolutionary War soldier. Dr. Pearce has said, "We must leap beyond what we know to invent that which no one else can conceive."

If he only knew how much I had conceived. How much I had risked. Not to mention, how much I had already leaped ahead in logic … and lunacy. I've survived the last two leaps by the skin of my teeth. As long as I've finally put things right—meaning Liam has survived—I will stop leaping. I will shut down my Leap Entanglement program.

At least, that's my plan. I still have no idea how I leaped this last time. The quantum quasicrystal still sits in its plastic case on the edge of the trellis. Perhaps I was too close to both the trellis and the quasicrystal at the twenty-one-hour mark and that's what sucked me into the past?

I'll work on that problem after I search up the aftermath of this leap.

Did Rasher survive?

With the wound in my side stinging, I crawl toward my chair and haul myself into it. My fingers graze the keyboard, but then I stare at the sticky note stuck to the bottom edge of the monitor. *A leap in time requires a leap of faith.*

The words are written in an efficient, slightly angled script. Not particularly feminine, but there were two women in here when I leaped. It doesn't seem like Akane Souza's type of sentiment. Based on our conversation about faith, this has to be a message from Torri.

Something about it strikes a chord deep within me. Not necessarily about God. But about how I believed I could change things when I leaped the first time. I had faith that I could save Kiefer, except then I lost Liam.

Is that what faith is like? Always being one step behind God, scrambling to keep up?

I shove my confusion aside and open my AI assistant app with shaking fingers. News about Rasher will have to wait because there is one thing I most want to know, and yet, it's what I'm most afraid to learn—does Liam exist in this timeline? I type *Liam Crosby* into the search bar of my app with shaking fingers.

My breath hitches as I read the article that comes up. Liam Crosby led the Boulder High School Panthers basketball team to a state championship victory over the Thunder Ridge Grizzlies. His all-time-high scoring record of thirty-six points made the difference in their 82-75 win.

Yes! I met him at that game. We both ended up on the All-Star Team, even though my Fossil Ridge High School team from Fort Collins didn't make it to the championships. When it came time to take the All-Star picture at the ceremony, I was wedged next to him to help hold the Colorado State flag.

I scroll halfway down the page to find the picture but no, this can't be. My heart pounds, threatening to break my ribs to escape from my chest. The picture is there, but I'm not in it. Not anywhere.

My door creaks open. I don't turn to see who has entered. My gaze is glued to the spot in the picture where I should be.

"You're here," the astounded voice floods my body with conflicting feelings.

Excitement to see her. Relief that she still exists and seems to know who I am. Anxiety over what she must be thinking. After leaving her the way I did, she could have rightfully reported me to the dean and washed her hands of me. Of course, my disappearance would be a hard thing to explain to any administrator. I temper my happiness at her arrival. Maybe she's just here to get answers before she walks away from this crazy mess.

I slowly spin in my chair and catch her wide-eyed gaze. "Torri—" My voice catches. I clear my throat and try again, but she beats me to it.

"You're here," she repeats. The joy that had briefly lit up her eyes is fading into wariness. "I didn't know when you'd be back."

My shoulders slump, and I let out a sigh. "Twenty-one hours is my leap limit."

She focuses on the bloody stain on my shirt. "Oh my gosh, what happened this time?"

A stunted laugh bursts from my lips. No matter the circumstances, it's good to have someone to share this craziness with. "Would you believe a serial killer punched me?"

She shakes her head with an unreadable expression. "What wouldn't I believe at this point?" She crosses the room and stops short in front of me. A quick touch to my neck. "Even your spider bite seems to be angry."

"Can I ask you a strange question?"

A half shrug. "I think I've got more of them for you, so why not?"

"Where did I tell you that I was from?"

"You didn't." She gives a wry grin. "I look up relevant info on any suspect before I visit their home, even my neighbors. Your file says your family lives in Colorado Springs. You went to Coronado High School."

Of course, she had to protect herself, even if my violation was just harboring an armadillo. In today's world, where everyone's criminal profile, or lack thereof, is linked to their CRASH device, she could have found out basic details about me in thirty seconds.

Except the data isn't usually wrong. "But I'm from Fort Collins. Lived there my whole life. We never moved. Coming to school in Boulder was my first time away."

She slowly shakes her head before her expression goes flat again. The woman has a seriously good poker face. "Your file indicates you moved from Fort Collins to Colorado Springs in 2040 when you were nine years old."

That would have been around fourth grade—about the same time my father went to prison. Perhaps my mom decided to get some distance from him? We didn't have much money, but maybe she borrowed some to get away from the area. The kids in Fort Collins had always been cruel about my having a conman father. She could have moved to help me. Odd that something like that would change based on what I did on my last leap.

At least Liam seems okay. Happiness washes over me, along with a strange sense of power, like I raised someone from the dead. Because I kind of did. Now that everything is right in my world, I just have to figure out how to stop leaping. Not only do I want my life back, but it's too dangerous to risk changing more events. Every leap is like playing Russian roulette with the universe. The next time, I could come back to a future I don't recognize at all.

CHAPTER 23

"Is there a first aid kit in the office somewhere?" Torri asks.

"In the break room. Cabinet above the fridge."

She nods, flicks her gorgeous hair over one shoulder, and goes to retrieve it. In her absence, I mull over my next steps. Do I tell Torri the whole truth? She deserves it, but will she believe it? Probably, after what she's seen.

I spin my chair in a circle. More urgently, I have to figure out how to stop myself from leaping in time. Akane must have done something to keep my program going. She has answers, but she likes to play games. Plus, she has no incentive to tell me.

By the time Torri returns, I'm no closer to a game plan. She kneels on the floor, since there are no other chairs in the room, and I swipe off the Gatchaman T-shirt. *Sorry that I never gave it back, Rasher.*

As she leans in, I catch a hint of floral perfume and a glimmer of interest in my physique, though she quickly hides her reaction. The spark is replaced with her professional medical persona. Perhaps she wasn't waiting for me here *just* to get answers.

Removing the gauze and cleaning the wound again with an

antibiotic wipe gives her the perfect reason to not meet my gaze. If only I could tell what she's thinking.

Finally, she asks, "Where were you?"

Her sharp glance and set jaw tell me that the direct truth is the only response she'll accept. She returns her attention to my wound.

Okay, here goes. "Montana in the 1970s."

That sharp glance spears me again, searching, trying to determine if I'm lying. I meet her gaze and hold it. I won't hide anything from her.

"You …" She twists her lips as if not sure how to say it. "You time traveled?"

I nod while running a hand through my hair. It feels strange to share this with someone in my home time.

"How?"

I take in a breath and launch into the explanation I would give in my doctoral defense. "Time is like a fifth dimension. Based on the quantum phenomenon of superposition—"

She holds up a hand to stop me. "No more nerd speak. Just tell me what's going on."

I wet my lips and begin again. "I've been studying time travel. Normally, I would have done more tests prior to acting on my hypotheses, but I started traveling a few days ago because Kiefer was killed by a guy named Seth Millstone."

She blinks at me several times. "The Kiefer I met the day before yesterday?"

"Yes. The nice guy you met was killed the day before that."

I launch into a full explanation of how I planned to "fix" things and stop Seth Millstone, but then I ended up in the Civil War and had to make hard decisions. I saved Kiefer but somehow lost Liam.

"So you wanted to restore Liam?" she asks. "Is that why you traveled this time?"

"Not exactly. I wouldn't have brought you into this by traveling in front of you. This time, it just happened."

"What caused it?"

"I have no idea. I need to scrub my computer program to find out what went wrong." As she finishes with the bandage, I reach over and pick up the case with the quasicrystal inside. "I didn't even have this with me."

She moves to sit on the base of the trellis. "Is that how you travel?"

"This, and the trellis. At least, that's what I thought."

She looks down at the floor and twists a ring with a green stone around a finger on her right hand.

"What is it?" I ask.

When she meets my gaze, her vulnerability pricks at my heart. "I saw the shock on your face and suspected you didn't mean to go. At first, the idea of time travel swept me away. But then I began to worry you might never come back."

I grapple for something to reassure her but come up empty. I don't know why I traveled, and just because the twenty-one hour rule has held twice now, I can't say for sure that will always be the case. And of course, there's the possibility I might die in the past. Clearly, I can't promise her anything. But it's heart-warming that she was worried.

I grasp her hand to still the ring twisting. We barely know each other, but now she's one of the few people who knows what I'm going through. That has created a bond greater than either of us is willing to admit.

I gently rub a circle on the back of her hand. "Just so you understand, I'm not trying to escape this time period. And you are one of the reasons I'd like to stay here."

Her gaze flicks to mine, and a hint of a smile graces her lips. "I took care of Myrtle and Artie for you. But I think Myrtle misses you. She lets me pet her for a few minutes, then she sits by the garage door and whines."

The change in subject throws me for a second. Guess we're done talking about relationship possibilities. "Yeah, she's pretty attached to me."

"At least, Artie doesn't think I'm a poor stand in for you. He gave me lots of cuddles."

Hmm. *Stand in.* The words resonate in the back of my brain. "A proxy," I murmur.

Could that be the answer to one of my questions? I flip my elbow up and stare at the CRASH device nestled in the crook. It's flashing the same purple and yellow polka dots that it displayed when I returned last time. Maybe it wasn't confused by the leap home as I'd assumed. Maybe it became attuned to the quasicrystal during the last leap, and in this one, it acted as a stand in?

Torri catches on without any more information. This girl is smart. "You think that's how you traveled?"

"It does have sophisticated AI embedded in it, only rivaled by the AI suite Dr. Pearce is working on."

"How do you stop it, then?"

"Good question. If it's attuned to the quasicrystal, then it must be drawing data from my computer program." I swivel to the desk and click my computer to life. "If I take out the input parameters, it won't have anything to hunt for, and I should stop leaping."

"What were your input parameters?"

"Seth Millstone's DNA." After highlighting the command pointing to the specific DNA profile, I delete the whole line of code. "That should do it. With no place to start, the program will fail to run." I turn my chair back to face her.

She furrows her brow. "You're sure?"

"The only other thing I can do is blow up my program entirely, and I'm not ready to do that."

A slow nod, but not in a way that's agreeing with me. "Maybe you should consider that for a moment." She puts a hand up. "Don't get me wrong. What you've accomplished is amazing and groundbreaking."

I pretend to fan myself. "Go on."

She gives a dry laugh. "But seriously. This technology could be a bigger risk to the world than when Oppenheimer's team invented the atomic bomb. You were working on this before Keifer was hurt. Why did you do it?"

She's touched a nerve without realizing it. The full truth gets stuck in my throat. And yet, I have to give her some version of the truth. I'll lay my own vulnerability out there and see what she does with it. "I can sometimes be a little extreme. If someone tells me not to do something, I'll do it just to show they can't control me, even if whatever they told me not to do is probably the better idea. As a scientist, I know it doesn't make sense to be so hardheaded and illogical, but sometimes I can't help myself. I wish I wasn't like that." I take a deep breath and blow it out in a rush. "I was drawn to time travel because it's the ultimate do-over. A reset, where when I'm busy proving how autonomous and stupid I am, I can go back and fix whatever I messed up."

She doesn't need to know that changing the things I've done is not the only end goal I've contemplated. I fantasized about being able to change my own past entirely. What would life have been like if I'd had the same mom but a different dad? What would I be in that case? Genetically, I wouldn't be the same me, but I'd probably be a better person without the Lockporte blood running through my veins.

"Hey, since you know my history, did you happen to hear the results of my dad's parole hearing that I missed?"

"What parole hearing?" She quirks her head. "Mars, none of your family has ever been arrested."

CHAPTER 24

I SHOOT TO MY FEET, almost tipping my chair over before realizing it and adjusting my stance. The implications of her words are careening around in my mind like a Ping-Pong ball. I open my mouth to tell her to give me a minute before she explains, but her words tumble out too fast.

"Your father has a clean record. There were some rumors he might be arrested, given that he wrote a book about how you had early onset dementia, but he claimed to believe it was true and to believe in the cure he sold. He called the whole thing an innocent mistake made by a nonmedical person. The police never had enough evidence of intent to bring fraud charges."

My jaw hangs like a dead weight. These are the heavy consequences of what happened in this recent leap. Years ago, my cousin Rochelle convinced me to turn my dad in and testify against him for defrauding all those people. Some of them gave half their life savings not only to help me fight a rare undiagnosed condition but also to get the cure for their own fight. She helped me get justice for them. I open my phone and search for her name in my genealogy quarto. Rochelle is still here. But of course, I took the phone with me, so why would it have changed?

I sink into my chair, swivel to my computer, and pull up my genealogy research saved there. The family tree lists my relatives one by one in a series of boxes. There is no box where her name or her father's name should be. Even so, I can't quite believe it. I do an internet search myself, no AI assistance. Only one Rochelle Lockporte exists—a sixty-year-old woman in Washington State. My Rochelle really is gone. Moisture wells up in my eyes.

She was an active, tell-it-like-it-is girl. One of my best friends growing up. I talked to her about all manner of things I couldn't tell my parents. The bullying at school. The crush I had on Hannah Romano. How it made me feel dirty when my dad used my name in a lie. Rochelle is the cost of stopping Brenda Morrow. Not just the theoretical loss of one human being, but the cost to *my* family.

While blinking to dispel the moisture in my eyes, I spin my chair back to face Torri. "What is my father doing now?"

The irony doesn't escape me. In bringing one family criminal to justice, I freed another.

"He runs a tech startup." Torri stands and pulls out her phone to check her reports. "It's called March Matrix. It purports to use special algorithms to analyze statistical data to model and predict brain patterns in consumers."

Brain patterns. Just like the modeling I did for Dr. Pearce. *Uh-oh.* The patent meeting. Did I miss it?

"March?" she asks. "Pretty close to Mars. Is the company named after you?"

"Not likely. I am named after the month, which was named after the god of war, but my father and I share a birth month, and he has always felt like we are at war with everyone around us. Take what you want first before anyone can take it from you. Survival of the fittest stuff."

"Sounds like a hard way to grow up."

She doesn't know the half of it. And, well, I guess I don't know the half of it now. My dad went to prison when I was eight in my timeline, so I must have lived the second half of a childhood in this timeline with him that I never lived before. How much of my childhood would have changed from what I remember?

She stands, places a gentle hand on my still bare shoulder, and holds up her phone to show me a picture. It's my father with his dark hair stylishly coifed into a wave over his left brow, wearing a dark blue suit and teal-colored tie.

"He's a billionaire," she says quietly.

"I don't believe it for a second."

"His company was just revalued—"

"No, I mean, I don't believe this is a legitimate business. It's his biggest con yet."

She looks at me quizzically.

"You saw the book in my house. I still have the book, don't I?"

"Yes. You're right. That had to be a con. No one could believe you have a degenerative brain disorder." She pushes her dark, silky hair over one shoulder. "But he must have gone legit. How could he con all those investors?"

"I don't know how, but he has. Trust me."

Her light brown eyes darken to amber as they focus intently on me. She's using her cop instincts to decide if I'm credible. A full body search would be less uncomfortable.

While she's making up her mind, I pull my T-shirt back on over my head. The bloodstains will get me some looks whenever I leave the office, but I don't have any other clothing here.

Finally, she gives an almost imperceptible nod and says, "Your father may not be your most immediate problem. Ellis told me Dr. Pearce is angry with you for missing a patent meeting."

"Ugh." Her sudden familiarity with my colleague, Ellis, barely registers as the thought of my mentor's wrath fills me with shame.

Before I can decide how to proceed, Akane Souza waltzes

into the room like she owns it. Her dark hair hangs loose instead of in its typical efficient ponytail.

"You," I growl. "What did you do to my computer program?"

Torri points her finger at Akane. "I also found her in your office while you were gone, doing something to the computer."

Akane backpedals a step, putting both hands up in a placating gesture. "The time loop is not my fault."

Anger vibrates through my veins. She doesn't even know what she's talking about.

"It's not a time loop. It's a leap."

"What do you mean?" Akane asks.

I roll my eyes before realizing I'm copying Morrow's habitual tell. "A time loop is where the same things keep happening over and over until you change something specific. This is nothing like that."

Her eyes widen in anticipation. "What's it like?"

"Oh, no. You're not debriefing me. You shouldn't even know about my project."

A momentary flash of disappointment mars her face, but it's quickly replaced by a smug smile. "Dr. Pearce sees everything done on the university computers. I've been in the *loop* on your project from the beginning."

Is she telling the truth? I assumed Dr. Pearce would be more professional and keep my work on time travel to himself.

I clear my throat. "Knowing is not the same thing as manipulating. Tell me what you did. Why did I leap without trying?"

"I don't know why you traveled this time. As for what I did, you'll have to ask Dr. Pearce."

CHAPTER 25

After kicking Akane out of my office, I leave Torri sitting in my chair to guard my computer while I try to track Dr. Pearce down. He hasn't made it in yet. In fact, his assistant, a young grad student named Dirk, says he's running late this morning and won't be in for several more hours.

When I return to the office, Torri looks up from her phone with a grateful smile, as if she thought I'd disappear again. She has no idea how much I wanted to get back to her.

Since I can't make any headway right now, she convinces me to go home and take a shower, maybe even cuddle with my animals, before coming back to confront the doctor. I need to look up what happened to everyone in Montana, but Torri is waiting and a shower sounds amazing after hiking all over the wilderness. At least I didn't receive as many new wounds as I had during my time in the Civil War.

Geez, it's a good thing no one can hear my internal monologue. Not yet, anyway. That potentiality is what the patent meeting was supposed to be about.

After I lock my office, Torri and I step out into a beautiful fall day, heading for the bus stop. I briefly touch her hand. "Thank you for being here when I got back."

"Well, it's not every day that a guy disappears before your eyes. Talk about ghosting me. I had to know what happened to you. I convinced Ellis to talk, not that he knew much."

"Bet that wasn't hard." I allow my gaze to sweep from her form-fitting light blue tank top to her hip-hugging jeans. "You would have him from *pretty please*."

A sweet blush creeps into her cheeks. "He could only tell me the basics of what you were working on, confirming what I could glean from your degree in applied physics with a specialty in temporal phenomena."

We don't have to wait long because the bus pulls up just as we reach the stop. The students who board are a rowdy group. They spend the ride hazing each other about girls, grades, and sports prowess. Nothing unusual, but a sudden pang of longing hits me. I have plenty of friends but few times when I've enjoyed such easy camaraderie. More often, I'm focused on making progress—my schooling, my projects, new sports, even the betterment of the human race. This intense need to prove myself has demanded a price I don't count often enough.

As we disembark, Torri takes a few steps toward her house, which is situated right in front of the bus stop. But I can't let her go so quickly. Every time I thought of coming home to this time-line, her face inspired me. I may not understand the connection between us, but I'm done questioning its existence.

"Do you need to get home right away? Or can you come over for a bit?"

Her smile is tinged with trepidation. "I can come over."

We walk to my house a few doors down. I enter the code on the garage door, then swipe my CRASH device to open the interior door. Right away, I see evidence of Torri's presence in my house—a new dog toy for my domesticated wolf and my father's book lying on the coffee table instead of in the empty bookcase. Kiefer had given her the guest code when I last disappeared.

Myrtle comes bounding out from the bedroom and slams into

me full force. I grunt as I absorb the hit and begin to scratch behind her hairy ears. "Hi, girl. I missed you too."

She sniffs intently as if she can smell Daisy or Pepper on me. It's wonderful to see my wolf hybrid, but I will miss Daisy's soulful howl. After a few seconds, Myrtle turns her attention to Torri, who rewards her with several more pets.

"Give me a minute to shower," I say.

Torri agrees, maybe a little too enthusiastically. Perhaps I need to use some deodorant as well.

While the water warms up, I check my phone contacts for Liam's name. Our last text exchange comes up regarding the time of the cutthroat basketball game we played on Monday. It seems like a lifetime ago. I scan down to his response, and it makes me shudder.

IF YOU HOG THE BALL THIS TIME, I'LL THROW IT
OVER THE CLIFF.

Almost a foreshadowing of the event that started all this—Kiefer being thrown off the cliff, then murdered on his way home from the hospital. But at least both Liam and Kiefer are alive, and we're all friends.

After a quick shower, I toss Rasher's *Gatchaman* T-shirt in the hamper and change into another one. This one has a picture of an otter holding a lightsaber with the caption "Using the force, I Otter be." Might as well wear my nerdiness on my chest, loud and proud.

Before I return to the living room, I grab my laptop and sit on my bed. I can't wait any longer for information. In the search bar, I type *Marvin Rasher Montana*. Who names their kid Marvin, anyway? That's just asking for a nickname like Marvin the Martian.

A birth announcement from November 1979 comes up.

Marvin Rasher, Jr., born on November 14, 1979, to parents Marvin

*and Ivory Rasher of Meadowlark, Montana. He weighed eight pounds,
seven ounces.*

A big baby for that time period. I let a smile creep up on my
face. Rasher didn't just survive. He married Ivory and started a
family. But that poor kid became Marvin the Martian, Jr.

I scroll down to find an earlier entry. An article in the Sula
Republic newspaper from August 31, 1972.

*Marvin Rasher is hailed as a hero for apprehending the perpetrators
and solving the case of twenty-one grisly murders of women and children. Before Ranger Rasher could take her into custody, Ranger Brenda
Morrow had already killed her partner in crime, Allen Lund, a hospital
lab technician. When confronted, Morrow stabbed Rasher, and he was
forced to shoot her. She survived and is due to stand trial early next
year.*

Rasher wisely made no mention of my presence at the scene.
Wonder what he thought as my body melted away.

I must not have hit Brenda directly in the chest like I'd
thought, since she survived as well. After clearing the search bar,
I type *Brenda Morrow Montana.*

Several articles from Montana newspapers come up. In the
end, she was convicted on twenty-two counts of murder. The
jury decided she played a part in the deaths of ten women and
ten girls, plus Allen and her first victim—her sister, Pamela.
However, they found there wasn't enough evidence to convict
her in the murder of Serenity Brooks. Too bad because she
clearly tried to set Rasher up for that one.

Brenda spent the rest of her days in a Montana State Prison
near Deere Lodge, Montana. She died in an inmate-related stab-
bing four years after her incarceration, never having married or
had children.

Thus, she must not have been a direct ancestor of mine or I

wouldn't still be here. I shift gears and access the genealogy quarto on my phone again.

I search for her name within the quarto. Sure enough, she was the daughter of Oliver Lockporte, who was a brother to my ancestor five generations ago. Nothing stood out as memorable about her life in my original genealogy research. That means she got away with her crimes in the previous timeline. Perhaps I did leap there for the purpose of stopping her crime spree. For the moment, I just add the note SK next to her name for Serial Killer. As I scroll down, the connection to Rochelle becomes clear. Morrow originally had a child out of wedlock who later took the Lockporte name—a child who was never conceived in this time-line because Morrow was in jail.

My thoughts turn to Gerald Morgan. Did Morrow really kill him like she claimed? A quick search of his name reveals nothing past 1972. For all practical purposes, he disappeared and his tita-nium mine slid into obscurity. My gut pinches tight. He might have escaped the area and changed his name, but the truth is probably simpler. Brenda and Allen killed him and stashed his body where it would never be found. Morrow could have tasked Allen with hiding Gerald while she went to the ranger's station to feign innocence.

I flip the laptop closed and return to the living room, only to find it empty. But the sliding glass door is open.

Torri is outside petting Artie, as much as you can pet an armadillo's hard shell. He rubs his snout against her leg, completely at peace. Funny, that's how she makes me feel as well.

I lightly touch her shoulder. "Wanna go for coffee?"

She grins up at me from her hunched-over position. "As long as you don't think this counts as a date."

Hopefully, she means I need to take her somewhere nicer for a first date, not that she won't go on a date with me. I twist my mouth to the side as if I'm thinking it over. "Deal."

The Sensitive Sipper coffee shop is just around the corner

from our residences. It specializes in food for people with food allergies and also supports important charity causes. I don't have food issues, but I'm all in for supporting charities … legitimate charities, that is. My stomach growls as we cross Broadway Street. When was the last time I ate? Plus, the change between my time and the leap time has totally messed up my internal clock. It must be about nine in the morning, but I can't keep my yawn inside. Hence, the coffee.

At the coffee shop, we both grab an empty mug and a pastry from the self-serve display case. I swipe my CRASH device on my elbow to pay for the food, then we move to a booth situated in a private corner.

I swipe my elbow again to authorize funds to turn on the coffee meter. The Environmental Rescue Act of 2045 outlawed disposable paper coffee cups in Colorado since those are a major contributor to landfill waste. Either patrons bring their own travel mugs or use the mugs provided at the shops. Thus, most coffee shops have gone to the spigot method of dispensing coffee to cut down on staff.

Torri turns on the spigot for milk and fills her cup partway before using the frother to make it foam. Then, she adds in the espresso and vanilla syrup from separate taps to make a vanilla latte. Typically, I drink tea since I don't like the taste of coffee, but this morning, I need all the caffeine I can get. I select the coffee spigot containing the strongest black coffee.

Now that I'm sitting still, staring at what will make me feel more alive—caffeine and food—guilt sets in. I get to enjoy these things while Rochelle does not. Perhaps I am destined to lose someone every time I leap. Playing God is no joke.

Torri places her hand on mine. "What is it?"

I tell her all about my time in Montana and then confess that Rochelle being gone is why my father is still free to spin his cons. "I wasn't strong enough to speak up on my own. I needed her to give me permission." I rake my hand through my hair. "Time travel doesn't have a trickle effect on the future;

it's a roaring cascade that sweeps the most meaningful stuff away."

She sits back and purses her full lips. So cute when she's thinking. I resist the urge to smooth a thumb along her bottom lip. As strong as this desire is, it's more important to find out what she's thinking about all this.

"It's human nature to want things to turn out for the better." She shakes her head. "You want your time in the past to have worked for good. All you see is that one person brought to justice caused another one to go free—your father—and eliminated Rochelle. But you can't trade one for another equally. Life doesn't work that way. As humans, we don't have the right perspective to tell if something has turned out better or worse."

The implication being that someone or something other than us has a more complete perspective. But what if there is no better perspective? I take a scalding swallow of coffee, savoring the burn as it goes down. "There's no way to know if I've done overall good, if this was a waste, or if I've hurt more than I've helped."

She gives a wry smile. "A truly honest answer. However, I believe God is working in everything, including what you've done."

"Are you saying God wanted my father to keep bilking people or for Rochelle to blink out of existence?"

"Of course not. But God is allowing you to change things in the past that are setting some things right. Morrow and Lund would have kept killing if you hadn't stopped them. Who knows how many people you saved. And obviously, you made big changes when you saved Long Browning."

She has a point. Long's descendant became the current, highly respected president of the United States.

"There's something I didn't tell you about my leaps. It sounds even more insane than the leaps themselves."

She sits straight up and puts her arms on the table, almost knocking over her coffee.

I steady it for her before explaining. "In each leap, I was confronted by a person who had a sort of body halo around them. In the first one, it was Long, but in the second, Allen Lund had the halo. Two opposite people, yet I had the strong desire to protect them both. What do you think it means?"

Her forehead puckers. "That is confusing. One seems totally innocent and the other completely guilty."

"Plus, I saved Long, but Allen ended up dying. Just before he died, the halo disappeared, along with the protective instinct. So, either I failed or it wasn't about protecting him in the first place."

She takes a long sip of her latte, mulling it over. Finally, she says, "Perhaps guilt versus innocence isn't the issue. What if it's about the changes that need to be made?"

A gong seems to go off in my head. Torri has hit upon something, but my tired synapses can't seem to pull it from the depths of my mind.

She wraps her hands around her mug. "Maybe you were supposed to help Allen change before he died."

The memory crashes into my mind with the force of a pinecone falling from a great height. Allen spilled a secret just before Morrow killed him. "I think it was his confession that mattered. Morrow's sister was the first victim. More than likely, no one found out about her death in the original timeline."

I grab my phone and type *Pamela Morrow* into the search bar. An article about the discovery of her body sits at the top of the list. A few lines in, a quote from her mother resonates like a tuning fork in my soul. "I'm so grateful to know she didn't run away from the strife in our family due to the divorce. I blamed myself for years after her disappearance."

When I share the quote with Torri, she grabs my hand and squeezes it. "I know it doesn't take away the pain of losing Rochelle, but this must be part of the reason why you see the halos." She bites her lower lip, as if she isn't sure whether to say this next part. In an awed voice, she continues, "God is communicating with you."

Is he, though? The skeptic in me can't quite go there. "It's probably just some random glitch in my mind caused by linking my quantum signature with people in the past."

She shakes her head. "If that were true, why didn't the halo appear on the people you would have been linked to by your genetics or by your computer program? Like Francis Millstone in your first leap or Ivory Gammon in this leap. Or for that matter, why not Brenda Morrow since you are directly related to her?"

I have no answer and merely nod to acknowledge her point.

But Torri isn't done yet. "I think the halo is meant to give you hope."

This throws me. "Protecting a serial killer is supposed to give me hope? I don't follow."

Her smile dazzles me as she answers. "In your leaps, the halos give you a problem to work, something to anchor you. The Bible says hope anchors the soul. Following the halos brings you hope that you can change things in the past for the better."

Her enthusiasm is infectious, so I return her smile. Even so, I can't quite cling to her theory—that God is using me to make the world a better place. The idea of an omnipotent all-powerful being reminds me too much of how I used to feel about my father. And look how that turned out.

I wince as I sip my coffee that is so strong it could masquerade as asphalt. Hopefully, the question of halos and leaps is moot, as I don't plan on traveling again.

CHAPTER 26

WE TALK for several more hours about everything besides time travel. Thank goodness. After I walk Torri back to her house, she finally gives me her personal cell phone number—a small but significant victory. She's on call tonight from 8:00 p.m. to 4:00 a.m., so she needs to take a nap this afternoon in case she's called out this evening to wrangle a stray dog or feisty raccoon.

A nap sounds fantastic, but I need to meet with Dr. Pearce first.

I squeeze Torri's hand and promise to call or text with any insights from the meeting. It's nice to be able to discuss this with someone outside of the lab, someone who isn't scheming to use my research or trying to one-up me in front of everyone.

It's almost noon. Surely, Dr. Pearce has made it in by now. I return home to throw down some more food for Myrtle and Artie, then I head to the bus stop.

As I stand waiting, I sneak glances at Torri's house. How fast can she fall asleep? Is she cuddling up with her own animals? I never even asked if she has some, but she must, given her love for critters. Well, I'll have plenty of time to get to know her soon.

While I'm trying to keep my mind from wondering what she wears to sleep, I'm distracted by a slow moving hybrid car in a flashy red color. The Environmental Rescue Act also outlawed personal commuting, forcing residents to take public transportation. Only police are allowed to drive. To see a personal vehicle in this neighborhood is rare on the level of seeing a unicorn with its horn stabbed through a pot of gold. But as always, wealthy residents found a loophole in the law. As long as they keep a cop on their payroll as a driver, they can use a personal vehicle at any time.

Why would this one be driving down my street? Not the kind of area where the high rollers hang out.

It passes the bus stop and parks just beyond it. The door opens, but no one comes out for a while.

Rather than continuing to stare, I turn to watch for the bus once again. What do I care about some rich guy and his business?

I pull out my phone and check my email. Odd that Dr. Pearce didn't try to email me to find out why I missed the patent meeting.

"Son." That voice sends shivers down my spine.

I freeze with my fingers hovering over my screen.

"Don't you think it's time to come back home?"

I don't know why I left home in this timeline, but I can guess. It probably had something to do with being manipulated and being forced to take advantage of innocent people.

Slowly, I inch my head degree by degree in his direction, giving myself time to accept what my eyes are seeing. Gone are the ratty sweatpants and oversized sweatshirt. He's wearing navy dress pants, a pressed taupe shirt, navy tie, and a tailored navy suit coat with a hint of taupe running through the subtle pattern. A breeze whips his coat, but it doesn't ruffle his dark hair, which is gelled into a stylish wave. Instead of a desperate criminal, he looks like a presidential candidate.

His expression is eager and open. But I can only see the sneer of the man who stole my ID and threatened me. I've seen him pushed to the limit, driven to the edges of madness. And in those moments, he will always choose himself over anyone else.

"This side project of yours has already brought us years worth of funding," he says. "I need you to follow up with the investors. Keep them happy and begging for more."

Oh dear God. I've been helping him all these years. Without Rochelle, I truly never had the guts to stand up to him. Well, that ends now.

I turn to fully face him. "It's more than a side project to me. I'm good at this."

"Of course you are. You're brilliant. But I need you on the business side of things."

The sound of tires lets me know the bus is coming around the corner. I take a step closer to the curb and shoot him a hard look. "Not this time."

The bus screeches to a halt, and the door swings open for me. I glance at the door, then back at him. If only I could believe he's different from my father in my original timeline. Circumstances can change someone's character—I've certainly proved that within myself over the last few days—but fancy cars and success tend to corrupt character, not enhance it.

I take the first step into the bus.

"You can't avoid me forever!" he calls.

As I find a seat in the back, I mumble, "Sure would be nice to find out if I can."

After the bus pulls out and snakes around the red car, I shake my head to clear it of all thoughts of my father. For now, I must focus on Dr. Pearce. We have a lot to figure out. Not only to understand how everything went wrong, ending up with me traveling accidentally, but also to discuss what to do with my new technology. Dreams of a Nobel Prize in physics have given way to imagining the disastrous consequences of allowing time travel for the masses. I'm not cocky enough to assume I'm the only one who could make the mathematical leap—pun intended —thus this technology needs to be safeguarded.

When I arrive, Dirk raises his eyebrows ominously. He tells me Dr. Pearce is in a meeting with the dean of the department. Whatever they are discussing, I don't want to get in the middle, so I ask Dirk to send Dr. Pearce my way when he's done.

Once in my office, I remember the promise I made to myself about putting more information on my phone in case this happens again. Theoretically, I shouldn't leap any longer since I took out Millstone's DNA as a target genome, but what if I'm wrong? Better safe than sorry. I create some large empty quartos to hold the data, then instruct my computer to initiate a download of all the critical historical events from several databases.

While that is chugging along, it's time to investigate what might be going on with my code. I pull up the file labeled Leap Entanglement, which houses the code I use to travel in time. I click on it and rename it Leap Launch to indicate this is my first set of code. Then, I copy the folder, rename the copy Leap Rework, and begin scanning the code to find anything that doesn't look like my original work.

Several hours pass before I look up to check the time. It's always that way when I get deep into a coding project. Two thirty already. Did Dirk forget to tell Dr. Pearce to come see me?

I rub my tired eyes. I'm going on more than a day with no sleep, and I'm fading fast. I'll need to go home for a nap myself soon. For now, strong tea from the break room should do the trick.

As I put my hands on the desk to push out of the chair, my gaze lands on a line of code a few lines down from where I left off. Every muscle in my body freezes. From line number 2121, the words *Dreamcatcher* and *Minerva* jump out at me.

Why would either of those terms be in here? Ellis is the one working on Dreamcatcher, my program to record dreams via brain waves in order to statistically determine if déjà vu is a real phenomenon. I'm not involved with it much at this point, though Dr. Pearce is involved because of the patent issues. I didn't include it in any part of my original code, but Dreamcatcher isn't what concerns me most.

Minerva refers to the powerful artificial intelligence Dr. Pearce has been creating, named for the Roman goddess of wisdom, counterpart to the Greek Athena, who, as a warrior, prefers strategy over brute force. Akane must have added it to my code. At Dr. Pearce's behest? One of them has some sort of strategy for doing this, a reason to slip these terms in.

The structure of the code points to Minerva as a data input. A line farther down also exports data out to Minerva, routed through Dreamcatcher.

What in the world? Akane wouldn't be brave enough to do something like this without Dr. Pearce's authority. If she input this code via his instructions, why would he route my coding through his AI?

Only one answer comes to mind: to control my program. To control my leaps.

As if summoned by my heightened thoughts, a quick rap sounds on my doorjamb, followed by the deep timbre of Dr. Pearce's voice. "Mars, we're overdue for a conversation."

"That is quite the understatement," I say as I sink back into my chair and turn my head to face him.

His light blue eyes seem as guileless as ever. The picture of a curious scientist, taking in the world and spitting out hypotheses, data, and interpretation. Is it real or a carefully crafted persona?

His slightly thinning dusty blond hair could use a haircut. Guess I've had him running around too much. Since I have no other chair, he perches on the edge of the trellis where Torri sat hours earlier. His short stature leaves him looking comfortable even while hunched over.

"You'll be happy to know I have settled the patent matter without needing your involvement."

"Okay, how? I thought the guy needed to hear from the inventor."

"I showed him the recordings of you and Ellis trying it out. While Ellis is falling asleep, you describe how it works and how you made it. That was enough for him." Dr. Pearce narrows his eyes at me. "Care to explain why you missed the meeting?"

"Uh, I had to go out of town suddenly."

He squints even harder. "Out of town?"

"Way out of town." I swallow and cough a little through my dry throat. "Unexpectedly."

The professor twists his mouth to the side as if tasting something sour.

Should I tell him? He might already know. Akane implied as much. Plus, having his AI connected to my program is sketchy at best, even if I can't figure out why.

"A few days ago, I caught Akane altering my code for the leap project, then a friend of mine caught her in here yesterday. Akane said to ask you about it. Do you know what's going on?"

"I asked Akane to take a look at your code, not to alter anything. You have unique coding shortcuts. I thought it would benefit her to learn from your examples. But she was supposed to ask you. I take it she didn't ask."

"No." But his explanation doesn't pass the smell test.

Akane could have only gotten independent access to my computer using a main access login, which Dr. Pearce would have given to her. Why wouldn't he just ask me for samples of my code instead?

I move the touchpad on my keyboard to wake my computer again, then point at the offending lines. "So why would she have added code that directs my program to access Dreamcatcher and Minerva?"

Dr. Pearce tilts his head as he leans forward to take a closer look. "I have no idea."

I scrutinize his face. He's paler than normal, but maybe he's been stressed by the patent issues or the mysterious meeting with the dean. He meets my gaze with raised eyebrows, reiterating that he has no idea how this happened. If he's acting, then he's an exceptional actor.

He waves a dismissive hand in the air. "It isn't a concern either way. Dreamcatcher is localized on Ellis's computer for his data analysis. And Minerva is currently offline. Whatever her reasoning, Akane's efforts have come to nothing."

Is he right? But then, what would be the point to doing it at all? To show me she could? Perhaps she wants me to feel vulnerable, to throw me off and gain an advantage over the competition. Seems far to go, even for extra grant money.

Akane is nothing if not shrewd and calculating. She's not as reckless as I am. If she went to the trouble to take the login codes without permission and do this on her own, she would have had a strong reason.

"I'm going to delete all this," I say.

"As is your right." Dr. Pearce stands to leave. "Just do me a favor. Next time you decide to disappear *unexpectedly*, send me an email so I'm not sitting in my ivory tower ignorant of what's going on."

"Yes, sir."

At the door, he turns his head back to glance at me. "And Mars, I can tell from your demeanor that you're heading in a good direction with your research. You still have that spark of curiosity. Keep doing what you're doing, because only you can."

A chill runs through me from head to toe and back again, bouncing around my body, just like the echo of his words in my head. They are so close to Long's words from my first leap. *Keep doing that which only you can do in the world.*

My two mentors used the same sentiment. A coincidence?

Maybe. Torri would probably say it's God speaking to me through them. But no, it has to be coincidence.

I'm too tired to think about this anymore. Time to get home where my wolf is waiting for me, and if I'm lucky, Torri's floral scent still lingers in the air.

CHAPTER 27

A CUTTHROAT BASKETBALL game haunts my sleep. I'm on the perilous court, no basketball in sight, standing near the high drop-off. The valley opens up before me, hundreds of feet below. This is the same place where I jumped to save Kiefer less than a week ago.

I try to back away from the height, but I run into someone behind me. A half turn of my head reveals a sneer and strawberry-blond hair escaping from tight braids. Brenda Morrow can't be here. I left her eighty years in the past.

Before I can protest or remind myself this is all a dream, she shoves me toward the cliff. Not hard enough for me to go over. Just enough to annoy me.

I dig my feet in as she creeps up behind me again. But this time, when I look over my shoulder, it's not Morrow.

It's Akane, with her dark hair in a high tight ponytail.

She smirks at me. Her voice comes out in a dream warble. "Good with physics. Bad with people."

She shoves me with both hands. My feet stumble and slide closer to the cliff. But suddenly, her words are important to me. More important than staying back from the edge. I turn to face her, but I don't make it all the way around. I end up sideways with her hands on my right bicep.

"So easy to fool," she says.

What the heck does that mean?

She gives one last Superman shove to my arm. I tumble over the cliff's edge. The air rushes past me, but my panic soon dissipates, and I spread my arms like wings, letting myself enjoy the rush of free-falling. This is a dream, after all.

Just before I hit the ground, I awake with a start in my bed at home.

I run my hands through my disheveled hair, still savoring the imagined wind. Myrtle lets out a groan of disapproval at the disturbance. I check the time on my phone. It's two o'clock in the morning, so I can't blame her.

I fell asleep around six in my sweatpants and T-shirt, yet eight hours of sleep hasn't left me rested. My body aches with the need for more. Even so, this dream nags at me.

It was no more real than any other detailed dream I've had when I know I'm dreaming. So what is it that's sticking with me?

Maybe it was her voice. Akane's sympathetic tone was not at all like her.

So easy to fool.

I can't go back to sleep until I figure this out. Who has fooled me? Bits of conversation from the day filter through my mind. Arguing with my father, who can't fool me because I don't believe anything he says. Ellis talking about how gorgeous Torri is, as if I hadn't noticed. And of course, my discussion with Dr. Pearce.

My brain perks up, as if my subconscious has shined a flashlight on the professor's name. His phrasing brought up the memory of Long's words from my first leap, but it wasn't just that. There was more. He also mentioned a name from my second leap. Ivory. *So I'm not sitting in my ivory tower …*

What's the statistical probability he would insert statements from both leaps in one short conversation? Pretty slim. But how would he know about those things? The only one who knows everything at this point is Torri, and she wouldn't have had time to tell Dr. Pearce about what happened in this most recent leap.

Unless his meeting was with her, not the dean. I shake my suspicions away. No, she has no connection to the department. But none of this is making sense.

Maybe if I go to sleep again, I'll have another breakthrough. I roll over and stroke Myrtle's rough fur. Cuddling up with her is almost guaranteed to make me sleepy.

AN INSISTENT RINGING invades my subconscious. No dream or feeling of flying. Just an annoying ring. One that doesn't stop.

I roll over and drag the pillow on top of my head. It can't be time to wake up yet.

The ringing phone begs to differ.

I press the pillow tight over my ears. Finally, it stops. I start to drift back to sleep, then jerk with a start as the ringing begins anew.

I throw the pillow off, disgruntling Myrtle in the process, and grab my phone. The display reads Psychic Lab instead of Physics Lab because Ellis thought he was funny when he borrowed my phone one day a couple of weeks ago. Who would be calling me from the lab at 4:07 a.m.?

I swipe to take the call. "Hello?"

No answer. Just the noise of machines whirring in the background. Computers? It sounds like the physics lab.

A sharp intake of a quick breath.

"Hello? Who is this?"

Still no answer.

"Why did you call? Twice?"

Nothing more. Not even a whisper of breath.

"I'm hanging up." And I do just that, then lay my phone on the bedside table.

Now that the phone isn't ringing anymore, it emits a gentle *ping*. One of the apps is alerting me to something. I lay my head down without the benefit of a pillow, still too tired to care.

The *ping* comes again, so I glance over. The quantum wave detection app blinks at me insistently, indicating quantum wave oscillations are coming together. It reads ninety-two percent— the highest I've seen yet for superimposed quantum waves.

My stomach bottoms out, and adrenaline rushes through me. The last time it alerted was minutes before I leaped back to the present. I quickly calculate the leap limit in my head. At 4:17 a.m., it will have been twenty-one hours since I returned.

More adrenaline surges in my system, waking me fully as fear creeps in. Am I about to travel again?

My first thought is to call Torri. Rather than second-guess the instinct, I grab my phone and click on her contact number. She was supposed to be on call until 4:00, so she wouldn't likely be asleep yet.

It only rings once before she picks up, sounding completely awake. "Mars, are you having time traveling jet lag?"

If only she knew. I check the time on my phone again. "No chance to explain how I know, but I think I'm seven minutes from leaping again. Can you take care of Myrtle and Artie for me? Maybe even run interference with Dr. Pearce, if possible?"

She doesn't respond to my questions, but the few words she does utter fill me with gratitude. "I'll be right there."

CHAPTER 28

AFTER HITTING the button to end the call, Torri rushes to her back door and slips her Birkenstock sandals on over her socks. Oops, almost forgot her keys and phone. With no pockets available, she holds them both in one hand as she goes out the garage door. She'd already changed into her pajamas—wide-legged pants with Christmas puppies on them and a long-sleeved T-shirt to match—but who's going to see her run three doors down to Mars's house?

Mrs. Austin, that's who. The widow who lives across the street must keep a vampire's schedule to be up at four in the morning. A light spills out of her kitchen window, which overlooks the street. Too late to turn back now. As she steps out, Mrs. Austin appears in the window. She waves while the woman stares open-mouthed. As she quick-steps down the sidewalk, she stiffens her spine. This is not a walk of shame, and Mrs. Austin should mind her own business.

The night—or rather, the morning—is cool and crisp, promising just the kind of day that's perfect for a long hike in the mountains. But could Mars be right? If so, he won't be here to enjoy it. He'll leap off somewhere to face another time period alone.

A small part of her envies the adventure of it all. To experience times in the past as more than mere words in a history book. But mostly, she worries about him—well, once she became convinced he was telling the truth. Believing his tale is a huge leap of faith, but even if she hadn't seen him shimmer into nothingness, her belief came down to the details. No one could make up the immersive experience Mars has had in both time periods.

Lord, I don't know why this is happening or why you would allow anyone to travel in time and change events. Help me and Mars to understand your purpose in all this.

As she walks up his sidewalk, his front door opens, and he ushers her inside with the hand tightly gripping his cell phone. To her surprise, as soon as the door closes, he wraps her in a fierce hug.

A feeling of calm certainty sinks into her as if it emanates from his strong arms. This is the closest their bodies have been. She leans into him, fitting her head in the crook of his neck. He smells clean and fresh, like bodywash, with a hint of canine. An intoxicating mixture, in her opinion. Could he be one of those special men who sleeps with his pet?

As if summoned, Myrtle bounds over and squeezes her way between their knees. She not-so-subtly pushes them apart.

"It's okay, girl," Mars croons. "She can tell I'm unhappy about something."

Torri glances at her phone. It's 4:15 a.m. Two minutes to go. Maybe? She drops her keys and phone on a table in the entryway, then bends down to spend a few seconds comforting Myrtle.

When she straightens, she focuses on Mars. "What can I do for you?"

The smoldering look he gives her melts her insides. "You've already done it." He clears his throat. "By being here."

"Why is this happening?" The desperation in her voice shocks her a bit. She's gotten wrapped up in this man's life in such a short time.

"I wish I knew. I took out the target genome and all of Akane's changes that I could find. So if I'm leaping, I don't know what's driving it. Maybe I set off some sort of cycle on my first leap without realizing it? It might end up being something random in my code."

Nothing is random with you, Lord.

A flicker of fear flashes through his eyes. The implications of another trip to the past turns her stomach. He might change something that has dire consequences for the future. He might get hurt worse than he has been. He might not come back at all. What if he can't make it back and she never finds out what happened to him? Never knows if he lived out a life in the past or if he met a horrible end?

His form begins to fade, like turning up the transparency on a photo. Soon, his body will be so faded it will be diaphanous like a ghost. Then, he'll dissipate as if he never existed, the quantum bits of him traveling far away from her.

She can't just watch it happen to him all over again. But what can she do?

Maybe she can interrupt the process? Somehow anchor him to the present?

While he still appears semi-solid, she reaches out and clamps a hand on his forearm.

"Stay with me," she whispers as solemnly as a prayer.

Then, she presses her eyes closed and tries to remain grounded. A burning sensation sweeps over her whole body. But she doesn't let go. She focuses on the feel of Mars's strong arm beneath her fingers. Will it be enough to keep him here? Or will she open her eyes to find him gone?

Before I even open my eyes, my mind is screaming that something is different this time. The pressure on my left arm hasn't ebbed where Torri grabbed me. Almost like she's still holding on to me. It must be an artifact of being touched while leaping.

I pry my eyelids apart. Before I can take in my surroundings, I focus on the beautiful sight before me and let out a sharp gasp. *Torri!*

She's here with me.

Her eyes blink rapidly, their velvety brown depths shifting in confusion. Finally, her eyes open wide. "How?"

Clearly, it must have been because she touched me during the transition. I stay silent since she's smart enough to figure that out.

Then, she fires another question at me. "Where are we?"

I tear my gaze from her and look around. A river the width of a football field flows behind us. Green grass sits beneath us. A laundry line has white shirts blowing in the breeze in front of a little clapboard house.

"We could be anywhere in any time period," I say. "We'll have to figure it out as we go."

Grief and joy go to war within me. I wouldn't wish this experience on Torri, but having her here has refreshed my spirit already. I'm no longer in this alone. On the other hand, I now have someone else to protect on this crazy roller coaster ride.

A door bangs open, and a woman in a long light blue dress with a petticoat emerges from the house. Other than at costume parties, no one in the country has seen that style of dress for a couple of centuries. Narrows it down a bit at least.

When she spots us, she spins to the wall of the house and grabs a rifle I hadn't seen. Makes sense. Two strangers land in her backyard wearing weird clothes, especially Torri whose pajama pants are likely confusing at best and scandalous at worst in this time period.

She levels the gun at me and takes slow steps. As she comes closer, I register her features. Either she's middle-aged or the sun has created more wrinkles than normal on her skin. Her hair is in a bun but not under a hat of any kind.

"Are ye spies?" she whispers, not in an angry or suspicious tone. More of an excited one.

Spies for whom? I open my mouth to answer her, then slam it closed, unsure which answer would be best.

The first moment in every leap seems to be the most precarious. Again, Long's words cycle through my mind. *Keep doing that which only you can do in the world.* Something has brought me to this place. Whether in 1862, 1972, or this unknown time period, I have to keep trying to make a difference. For my sake. And now, for Torri's.

I look the woman full in the face and whisper back, "Aye."

SITTING ALONE in his office above the physics lab, Dr. Calvin Pearce checks the time: 4:21 a.m. Mars should have traveled by now. Hopefully, waking him up with a phone call gave him time to get dressed before he leaped. A small courtesy, but not the real reason Calvin had called. Since Mars is the first time traveler, there is no data to speculate about time travel while unconscious. Best not to chance it.

Calvin checks the tracking device on Minerva, then fires off an email to Akane Souza.

Traveler is in Colonial America, Long Island, New York. Analyze changes to timeline as data comes in for the next twenty-one hours.

No signature included. Signing an email is a waste of time, but some professors enjoy seeing PhD after their name every day. For most of them, the three little letters indicating their doctorate are probably the only noteworthy thing they will do in their lives.

He clicks on *send* and pushes the chair back from his computer. His work is done for several hours. Even with her limited knowledge of Mars's project, Akane will understand what to do when she comes in later today.

Time to go home to his family, such as it is. He and his wife, Isabella, live mainly as companions, not lovers. Those are the true consequences to marrying a completely opposite personality. Where Calvin is serious and driven to achieve, she is fun-loving and flighty. She cannot take his ambition seriously, and he cannot take her seriously at all. And yet, her spontaneous qualities that bolster the wall between them make her an ideal mother. She can adjust to a child's whims on the fly, parenting differently for each nanosecond of emotion that constantly pours out of their daughter, Emmy.

Not even Ryker's vicious temper tantrums can make her yell. She merely looks in his tear-filled eyes and says, "Screaming is not the way to get what you want."

For the sake of the children, they will stay together. Besides, their arrangement works out well. When he must stay at work into the early hours of the morning, she doesn't worry or complain about his absence. They thrive in their separate realms.

Similar to how Calvin has had to keep aspects of this project separate from the others. Mars is just now figuring out there's more to his project than he's assumed. And though Akane massages the data through Minerva, she has no idea how the AI program works. Or that Calvin records everything in Mars's leaps via a download from his CRASH device when he leaps back. The CRASH device receives brainwave data from a minuscule implant at the base of Mars's skull. It was designed to be smaller than a mosquito's proboscis. Mars never felt it go in. That data is then rendered in 3D by running the recorded brainwaves through the Dreamcatcher program.

The small deceptions Calvin has had to employ are necessary. If Mars had an inkling that the "missions" were planned and orchestrated, he would balk at such intervention—except to save someone he loves. No one wants to mess with the past until tragic events befall a person who actually matters to them.

That's exactly the reason why humans can't be trusted with time travel. We will only work in our own self-interest. We need a logical superintelligence to guide us into making the best decisions for everyone.

In the end, Mars's struggle will all be worth it to discover what an AI-driven future can look like. An excited flutter jostles Calvin's stomach. No more chaos. No more wars. No more human faults and failures. Only pure logic working out the future for the best of humanity. What a glorious future it will be.

FUN FACTS

- Meadowlark, Montana is a fictional town located in the Bitterroot Mountains near Sula, Montana (a census designated place with only about 40 residents) in Ravalli County. I chose the name Meadowlark to honor the state bird of Montana.
- Richard Nixon's nickname of "Tricky Dick" came about not because of the Watergate scandal. He first received the nickname in the 1950s congressional race because he created an ad without his political affiliation on it. This was perceived as trying to trick Democrats into voting for a Republican.
- Ivory's last name is Gammon to honor Sarah Gammon Bickford, a former slave turned business owner who settled in Virginia City, Montana. Not only did Sarah endure the death of two children, she suffered domestic abuse from her first husband and sued him for divorce, winning custody of their third child. She would unfortunately lose that child too, then remarry, have four more children, and finally take over the family business after her second husband's death. She

was a true, enterprising pioneer woman who survived many tragedies and still moved forward with courage.

- The scrunchie was around in the 1970s since it was first invented in 1963 by Philips E. Meyers, but it wasn't patented. The hair tie didn't become a popular trend until 1987 when nightclub singer Rommy Revson was looking for an alternative to metal hair ties. She patented her elastic invention, which was inspired by the elastic on her pajama pants.

- The massacre that Ava Millstone finds herself involved in was inspired by the Marias Massacre, an atrocity committed by the US Army in 1870. Due to the murder of a white man and fueled by the general hatred expressed for Native Americans by army officers, a group of soldiers opened fire on a peaceful camp of Native Americans, killing mostly women, children, and elderly. Those involved in the massacre received no official punishment.

- The Sawtooth Creek mine was a real titanium mine, now abandoned, near Hamilton, Montana. I couldn't find records for what years it operated or the name of who actually owned it, so please forgive my artistic license.

- The sweet dog Daisy is named for a beagle mixed with a blue heeler that is owned by a friend of my daughter's (you know who you are, Eliza). And Pepper is named for a dog we used to have as a kid (the counterpart to my white mouse named Salt—so creative).

- Pine cones from the ponderosa pines in Montana are not the biggest pine cones—they only grow to be around five inches long—but they can fall from a height of over 150 feet, thus giving them sufficient gravitational force to stun someone on the ground.

- Authors are not perfect. Did you notice the mistake in the series? When I started the first book, *Twenty-One Stones*, I forgot to look at what day of the week September 17, 2051 would actually be. Thus, I started the series on a Monday in my fictional world, when that date will happen on a Sunday in the real world. But for consistent story time, I've left it this way. Thus, the whole series is running a day ahead. How's that for time travel?

AUTHOR'S NOTE

I can't thank you enough for taking this leaping journey with me. Being able to share characters like Mars and Torri and their stories with you brings me such joy. I meant for Mars's adventure on this trip to be a fun murder mystery. If you figured out who the second killer was, good for you! If not, don't feel too bad. Most women aren't killers … most. Either way, I hope you enjoyed the tale.

If you have a minute, I'd love for you to leave an honest review on any site that hosts books: Amazon, Goodreads, Barnes and Noble, Bookbub. I read each and every one of them, even when they aren't at the top of the scale. I truly want to know how you think and feel about my stories.

And if you'd like to connect more with me (including give-aways, contests, and what books I'm reading), please sign up for my quarterly newsletter at https://janiceboekhoff.com. I would love to hear from you.

Blessings,
Janice

ACKNOWLEDGMENTS

Who can walk through life alone? Certainly, not me—I would never find my car keys. Truly, life is meant to be lived together with imperfectly perfect people doing chronically interesting things.

- Todd: what a life we have made together! We both get to do that which we were made to do and share it with each other. I couldn't ask for anything more.
- Zach, Jenna, and Riley: you have no idea what a blessing you are to your mom and dad. Through the ups and downs, we never quit on each other. I am so proud of each of you and the wonderful people you are growing up to be.
- Crystal Joy and Amelia Judd: you are such amazing writers and friends. My life is so much richer with you in it.
- Carol Brandon, Donna Feld, Mary Johnson, and Lisa Lee: I wait for your comments as a runner waits for the starting blast of the gun. Once a novel gets your input/tweaks, I know I'm on the right track. Thank you for being excited to be the first to read each novel.
- Kim Mesman: you are the best kind of designer—one who can take my muddled ideas and show me the best parts of them.
- Linda Yezak: you not only make my novels better, you keep me on track in writing them. My standing editing

appointment with you makes sure I keep working on my own projects. Otherwise, I would get lost in editing for other people. Thank you for your accountability, honesty, and encouragement.

- My Lord and Savior: thank you for bringing me to this point where I can write with freedom and security because your arms are always surrounding me.
- Wonderful readers: knowing that you are out there and that each of you reacts differently to the words I put on the page is a miracle to me. I hope that every one of you takes away from my novels exactly what you need at that moment. Laughter, thrills, adventure, faith, whatever you are looking for, I pray the Lord helps you find it.

ABOUT THE AUTHOR

Carol and Christy Award finalist Janice Boekhoff (pronounced Beau-cough) is a former Research Geologist turned Author. Although she's not nearly as tan anymore, she enjoys spending time in her office, dreaming up ways to kill a dinosaur or bend the fabric of time, with her Vizsla writing partner snoring in his dog bed next to her. A Midwest native, she writes from Iowa where traffic is nonexistent and hogs outnumber people 7 to 1 (good thing they can't drive).

ALSO BY JANICE BOEKHOFF

Twenty-One Stones (Leap Limit Book 1)

Jurassic Judgment Series

Earth Hunters Series

For info on new releases, freebies, and to see what I'm reading, please sign up to receive my quarterly newsletter at https://janiceboekhoff.com.